Bridge
An easy guide for beginners

The Intelligent Card Game
for Managers & Aspiring Managers

Prof. (Dr.) Hemant K Abhyankar

VISHWAKARMA
PUBLICATIONS
VP

Bridge An easy guide for beginners

The Intelligent Card Game
for Managers & Aspiring Managers

First Edition - August, 2016
© **Author**

ISBN 978-93-85665-47-9

Published by:
Vishwakarma Publications
283, Budhwar Peth, Near City Post, Pune- 411 002.
Phone No: (020) 24448989 / 20261157
Email: info@vpindia.co.in
Website: www.vpindia.co.in

Cover Design, Typeset and Layout
Chaitali Nachnekar

This book is dedicated to my parents

Late Sou. Snehlata & Keshav Ramchandra Abhyankar
who taught me bridge since 1959

&

My Guru Late Prof. Makarand Vaman Joglekar (Bosch)
(Ex. Principal, RIT, Islampur)

&

My Bridge partners

Late Prabodh Vishwanath Kulkarni
Late Kisan Rambahu Joshi,
Late Pramod Karmarkar

&

Mrs. Chitrarekha (My Wife)

They have all contributed to the development of this
"Engineering System".

From the Author's desk....

It was in 1959 that my parents invited me and my younger brother to play bridge. I was in the seventh standard and my brother, in the fifth. There was no written convention. The rules for bidding were dictated by my father and were frequently changed to suit him, without considering the arguments made by my mother. It was a great fun!

My mother was a real teacher to us for this game. She loved the game very much and played till the last breath, even though she was suffering from cancer and her lower limbs were paralyzed.

We continued to play bridge and learned the elementary systems like "Phoney Club", "Standard American", etc. We used to play "Rubber" bridge all the time. It was in 1975, that Sangli District Bridge Association was established and we started playing "Duplicate Bridge" regularly. As the founding members of the association, we took a lot of initiative to promote and expand bridge as a popular card game in households of Sangli.

Bridge gave me an opportunity to work as a tournament director at National level competitions and enjoy playing with the then stalwarts like Orlando Campos, Jimmy Mehta, Dr. Tibriwalla, Dr. Tolani and many such others.

My seniors helped me introduce this game to the students in the hostels of Walchand College of Engineering, Sangli. It was told to me that gambling in the hostels, by playing three cards or Rummy, was wiped out, once we introduced this game. Some of the students were asked questions only regarding the system of their bidding in Bridge, during personal interviews and they got selected for their dream jobs.

I sincerely thank Shri. Rajkumar Agarwal, Hon'ble Chairman and Shri Bharat Agarwal, the Managing Trustee of Vishwakarma Institute of Technology, Pune for permitting me to introduce this game in our curriculam.

I also thank Shri. D. D. Ghule and Mrs. Poornima Pawshe as both of them helped me in preparing the course materials first and then the latter worked only on this book to bring it in the current status. Typing without knowing A-B-C of bridge in very tough.

Shri. Vishal Soni not only followed up with me but has shown great patience as I did delay the checking and rechecking of this script, due to my hectic schedules.

I welcome all the readers to the wonderful game of bridge, which will allow them to keep their body and mind fit even beyond the age of ninety.

Prof (Dr.) H. K. Abhyankar

Foreword

B ridge is considered to be a very old and prestigious card game. Many persons have introduced various bidding systems like Culbertson, Goren, K. D. Joshi, etc. Many a players have used a system called "Precision" designed by a Chinese engineer. At top level, systems like Italian Blue Club, Forcing Pass, etc. have also been popular.

Having studied many of these systems, my Guru, Late Prof. Makarand Vaman Joglekar, who was my Partner for some years, suggested introduction of a new system in 1977. Both of us worked on this system and tried this system for many years. My other partner Late Shri. Pramod Karmarkar and I played with this system and won many laurels. While practicing, we made many changes. A written down script was never made available to others, although, I must have taught this system to hundreds of players.

We boldly introduced many indoor and outdoor games along with Yoga, as a part of our autonomous curriculum for our engineering students - "A Joyful Learning Model", leading to all round development of the students at Vishwakarma Institute of Technology, Pune in 2008. Bridge, as a Management Card Game, was introduced as a part of the curriculum and the first written script was prepared as a course material for my students. More than 300 students learned the game as a part of the curriculum in a couple of years.

It gives me a great pleasure to introduce this "Engineering Bidding System" to the already existing number of systems. It is only with the practice of this system that a correct contract could be reached even if you change the partner but use the same system. This has been proven while conducting weekly tournaments for the students. I am sure the readers can easily understand the system and can enjoy playing bridge on their own.

Prof. (Dr.) Hemant K. Abhyankar

Contents

❏❏❏

BRIDGE PLAYERS

KNOW
THEIR
PROBABILITIES

Bridge
An Intelligent Card Game For Managers

1.1 Introduction

- Bridge is considered to be an intelligent card game, free from card luck, hence it does not come under category of gambling.

- It is a game of four persons on one table. Two persons seating opposite to each other on one axis play as partners against opponent pair seating across on the perpendicular axis.

- It is a game of communicating your cards to your partner, in a code language – called "bidding system".

- Through this code language, you are supposed to arrive at a 'goal', in terms of 'tricks' to be made, known as 'contract'.

- If a card is laid face up by one of the players, all players play a card from their hand of the same suit. Ace is the highest card and two is the lowest card.

A card, which is highest, played by a player, is said to have won a 'trick' when all the four players have played the card of the same suit. In case if a player does not have a card of the suit already played, then, the player has an option to play a trump card, if any, to win a trick.

- There are graded incentives for specific contracts called as 'part - game', 'game', 'rubber', 'little slam' and 'grand slam'.

- Since communication among partners is equally understood by the opponents, there is a challenge to fulfill the "goal" proposed (contract).

- Your skill is to fulfill the goal by earning enough tricks, as stated in the 'final contract', whereas the opponents have an opportunity to defeat your contract by legally accepted methods of signaling and ensuring your pair does not make enough tricks which are necessary to fulfill the contract.

- This allows all players to learn principles of management, group work, communications, etc. and get an opportunity to fight with each other psychologically.

- While you play and learn, you get so much involved that you enjoy the feeling of meditation.

- After a long day of physical work, if you play bridge even for half an hour, your mind and body will be totally relaxed. It relieves you of physical as well as mental stress.

- So come! Let's play, learn and enjoy!

- That is the motto of 'joyful learning'.

1.2 The Background

- In a pack of cards there are thirteen cards of each suit, indicated by a sign i.e. S - Spade (♠) , H - Heart (♥), D - Diamond (♦) and C - Club (♣).

- Ace, King, Queen and Jack are considered to be pictures and other cards have serial numbers two to ten.

- This is a game to be played by four players. Two players sitting opposite to each other are partners and opponents occupy chairs on other axis of the table as opposite pair. The axes are generally called as North-South and East-West.

- The fifty two cards from a pack – excluding the 'jokers' are shuffled and distributed equally by a 'dealer' from left to right, in a clockwise manner, one card at a time, facing down.

- Each player has thirteen cards with a distribution, which would be statistically unique in entire life time of a player, even if one plays regularly. That is why the game is very interesting. You deal with a situation which is definitely new every time.

- In this text, a communication system is described which is designed by the Author and his Guru Late Prof. Makarand Vaman Jogalekar, after practicing it for over two decades.

- This system shall be called as 'Engineering System'. Many other systems exist all over the world, like Phoney Club, Standard Goren, Strong Club, Blue Club, Precision, etc.

- So, Come! Let's play and enjoy while we learn the system.

1.3   The Beginning

- When the cards are dealt, the dealer has first right to open a bid as per his/her own bidding system. The bidding then moves from the dealer to the Left Hand Opponent (LHO), then to the Partner of the dealer and then to the Right Hand Opponent (RHO) and back to the dealer, in a clockwise manner. It continues till three players consecutively bid 'pass' or 'no – bid'. The last call made, previous to the three consecutive pass bids, stands as a final contract. If all the players bid pass only then there is no contract and hence the cards are to be shuffled and dealt again.

- While bidding, every player has to use the same code words, described in section 1.7.

- When it is your turn, you may bid a suit at same level (one, two, three, etc., i.e. one Club, one Diamond, etc.) if it is of higher order in hierarchy than the one called earlier in the auction. The highest suit is 'No Trump' then ♠ then ♥ then ♦ and finally ♣ which is the lowest in hierarchy.

- If, at your turn, the suit which you want to bid is lower in hierarchy than the one bid earlier in that auction, then you have to bid your suit at at least one level higher than earlier bid. e.g. It is your turn to bid and somebody has bid '2 ♥' earlier in the auction then you will be allowed to bid a Spade or No trump at level two but if you wish to bid Club, Diamond or even Heart suits, then, you will be permitted to bid them at level which is at least one level higher i.e. 3 ♣, 3 ♦, 3 ♥ or more than '3' level too.

- The bidding stops if all the four players bid 'pass' or if there are three consecutive 'pass' bids after a last call.

- The last bid (call) is called as the final contract, as stated earlier.

- The player who first bids the suit of the final contract, during that auction, is called as a 'Declarer'.

- LHO of the declarer takes a card out of his/her hand and puts it face up in the middle of the table. This card is called an opening lead.

- When an opening lead is made all cards of the partner of the declarer are put on the table, all face up, properly arranged suit-wise with a Trump Suit to the left of the declarer. These are the cards of a 'Dummy', a name given to the partner of the declarer. Dummy is supposed to play cards only as directed by the declarer. The Dummy should remain silent, without making any suggestions or asking questions, during the play till all thirteen cards are played, i.e. the Dummy must remain silent till this hand is played.

- Note that while partners use a unique bidding system, the opponent pair may bid as per their own bidding system, which could be entirely different.

1.4 Winning a Trick

- When the opening lead is made, the declarer directs the Dummy to place a card of same suit, selected (indicated) by the declarer, at the centre of the table.

- Then RHO of the declarer plays a card of same suit from his/her hand and put it at the centre of the table.

- Declarer also selects a card from his/her hand of the same suit and puts it at the centre of the table. This is called 'following a suit'.

- These four cards, placed (played) face up on the table, one from each hand constitutes a 'Trick'.

- The highest card of same suit wins the trick.

- If one of the players does not have a card of the suit played on the table, he/she can play a trump card, if there is any, and win the trick, called as 'Rough' or he/she can play a card of any other suit, which is called as 'Discard'.

- The player who has won the trick plays the next card and others follow the suit in a clockwise manner. The next four cards constitute the next trick and the game continues till all the thirteen tricks are made.

1.5 The Bidding System : A means of communication

- Let us first learn how to evaluate your hand.

- Ace has four, a King has three, a Queen two and a Jack has one count (high cards points - HCP) for valuation.

- Ace being the highest card of each suit, will always win a hand or trick if that suit is played. Hence Ace is counted as one 'trick'.

- A King is next highest card of each suit and may win a trick, if Ace is not played, hence it is counted as a "half-trick".

- Ace and King together of the same suit in a hand are to be considered as "two-tricks" where as an Ace and Queen of the same suit together in a hand would be counted as "one and half trick". However, a King and Queen of the same suit together in a hand is considered to constitute "one trick".

The Beginning:

- A left hand opponent (LHO) shuffles the cards and gives it to you for a deal. The Right Hand Opponent (RHO) cuts the pack into two and you deal from your left hand opponent in a clock-wise manner till all cards are distributed, one at a time and face down position.

- When the cards are dealt by a dealer to you, first count the number of cards, which must be thirteen. Then arrange them in a descending order for each suit i.e. Spades, Hearts, Diamonds and Clubs.

- Put and arrange the cards closer to your chest so that neither the opponents nor your partner can see them. So, no information is leaked to others like which pictures you have or how many cards of each suit you have.

- Count your pictures and make a summation of HCP assigned to the picture e.g. if you have four Aces you have four pictures and sixteen HCP.

- Now, you are ready to communicate in a legally accepted language, called as 'Bidding'.

- So, Come! Let's play and enjoy while we learn more.

1.6 In short

Each Ace   is Four HCP and one trick

Each King   is three HCP and half trick

Each Queen is two HCP and no trick

Each Jack   is one count and no trick

However -

An Ace & King of same suit together in a hand constitutes seven HCP but two tricks.

An Ace & Queen of same suit together in a hand constitutes Six HCP but one and half trick.

And

A King and Queen of same suit together in a hand constitute five points and one full trick.

Remember:

- each suit has four pictures, which sum to ten HCP.

- there are four suits in a pack hence sixteen pictures and forty HCP.

- if HCP are equally divided to all four players, each one will get ten HCP.

- if pictures are equally divided to all four players each one will get four pictures (like A, K, Q, J or could be Four Aces or Four Jacks too).

- since you shuffle, cut and deal the cards each time, the distribution of cards, HCP, pictures and tricks to each of the players goes on varying from deal to deal and you will never come across the same distribution or same hand any time in your life.

1.7 Objectives of a Bidding System

a. Before we learn more about this calling system (Engineering Bidding System) let us understand how to decide the objective or a goal for bidding the final contract.

b. All bidding systems should use the same code words, which may have different interpretations but indicate the same contract.

The standard codes include –

i. Numbers one to seven, which indicates level of a bid, increasing with number.

ii. Names indicating suits i.e. Club, Diamond, Heart, Spade and No-trump (indicating No suit is a trump suit.)

iii. 'Pass' or 'No Bid' indicating disinterest in bidding at that turn.

iv. 'Double' indicating a challenge to defeat the opponent's contract.

v. 'Redouble' indicating readiness to fight and win over opponents who have challenged a contract by 'Doubling' it.

vi. 'Alert' – It is a call, which must be given by you, out of your turn, as soon as your partner, in his or her turn, makes a call, which is Artificial and not Natural. Alert call should also be given by a player, if he/she is going to bid a call whose level is one or more levels above than what is required at current bidding level.

c. Note, when you bid one Club, you are communicating with your partner to describe your hand. If this bid communicates strength and length of Club suit, then, it will be a Natural Bid. However, if it may not necessarily have to do anything with the Club suit, then, it is an Artificial Club Call.

d. Also note that if the final contract is one Club (for example), irrespective of the system you use, then trump suit is ♣s and the declarer will have to win six (datum) plus one, i.e. seven tricks with Club as a trump suit.

e. Similarly, a final contract of 3 No-trumps would mean

the declarer has to win six plus three, i.e. nine tricks without any trump suit.

f.   This means a final contract can go up to seven-level, which is known as a 'grand slam' and all six level contracts are known as 'little slam'.

g.   There is a fixed hierarchy of suits in this game. It is No-trump (the highest), ♠, ♥, ♦ and ♣ (the lowest) in descending order, as mentioned earlier.

Thus a bid of one ♠ is higher than a bid of one ♥ and a bid of two ♣s is higher than a bid of one No-trump.

h.   In the game of 'Bridge' two suits i.e. Club (♣) and Diamond (♦) are known as 'Minor Suits' and other two suits i.e. Spade (♠) and Heart (♥) are known as 'Major Suits'.

  i.   If you bid and make your contract you earn points as follows :

•   20 points per trick, bid and made, in ♣s or ♦s i.e. for Minor Suits.

•   30 Points per trick, bid and made, in ♥s or ♠s i.e. for Major Suits.

•   40 points for the first trick bid and made in No-trump contract

•   30 points for each additional trick bid and made in No-trump contract.

j.   The objective of any bidding system is to communicate with the partner, in legal language coded with numbers and suits, to evaluate joint strength of hands for arriving at a final contract,.

k. The strength of a hand means the high card points or HCP, lengths of suits, quality of suits (i.e. number of high cards of the suit), etc.

l. If the combined HCP of you and your partner is more than that of the opponents then you may bid and make contracts to earn points.

m. Stronger hands can bring in more points if you bid and make a 'Game or Rubber' or a 'Slam'.

n. The bonus for 'slam' is as follows :

Little Slam   :   Not vulnerable 500 points, vulnerable 750 (Twelve Tricks) points.

Grand Slam   :   Not vulnerable 1000 points, Vulnerable (Thirteen Tricks) 1500 points.

o. A 'game' means to earn a minimum of 100 points in one or more consecutive deals without an interruption of a game by the opponent pair. The pair which earns a game is said to have become "vulnerable".

p. To earn a 'Rubber' in contract bridge means to bid and make two games before opponents do so.

q. If a side makes two games with opponents not making a game in between then bonus is 300 points. However, if a side wins a Rubber by two games to one then bonus is 500 points.

r. Remember, in general you require following joint strengths, in a deal, to bid and make following contracts :

i. 24 – 26 HCP for a game in ♥s or ♠s i.e. 4 ♥ or 4 ♠ contract.

ii. 26 – 27 HCP for a game in No-trump i.e. 3 NT contract.

iii. 28 – 30 HCP for a game contract in Minor suits i.e. 5 ♣ or 5 ♦ contract.

iv. 30 – 32 HCP for a 'Little Slam' i.e. 6 ♣, 6 ♦, 6 ♥, 6 ♠ contract.

v. 33 – 34 HCP for a 6 NT contract. (Not more than one Ace or King missing from your hands)

vi. 36 – 37 HCP for a 7 NT contract (all Aces with you)

vii. 33 – 36 HCP for a 'Grand Slam' in suits provided you have a total control in all suits i.e. Aces and Kings or void in side suits.

viii. Even with ten HCP, you may be lucky enough to win all thirteen tricks if you have all thirteen cards of same suit, in a suit contract of same suit.

1.8 Bids are called "Natural Bids"

if they mean to show strength in a suit which is bid, i.e. if a bid is 1 ♥, its natural meaning would be the bidder wants to make seven tricks with ♥ as a trump suit (ref. 1.7.c)

However many bidding systems use natural bids either to communicate additional information or totally different information than the natural meaning. Such bids are called as 'Artificial Bids', and they need to be brought to the immediate notice of the opponents by tapping the table and giving out of turn 'Alert' call by the partner of the bidder as described earlier.

1.9

Many systems incorporate HCP/points for lengths of suits, however, 'Quality' of a hand remains in pure judgment of an individual player, which will be discussed later.

❑❑❑

Special Tip 1:

- Get a pack of cards Shuffle and distribute the cards to four (imaginary) players on the table.

- If you are four players, then start bidding.

- If you are alone, see one hand at a time and bid according to Engineering system.

- Refer the book frequently. It will help you learn faster.

- Check the bidding with reference to the book, and discuss with your partner and opponents.

- Arguements allow you to learn more.

2

BRIDGE PLAYERS

KNOW
THE SECRET TO
LONGEVITY?

Engineering System
Opening Calls (Bids)

- When one of the partners, on his or her turn, first makes a 'bid', other than a 'pass', it is called an 'opening call' or 'opening bid'.

- The right to bid first is to the dealer and then the bidding cycle moves from the left-hand opponent of the dealer to the right hand opponent, through his/her partner, and then back to the dealer, in a clockwise manner, and it continues in the same manner till a final contract is reached. A final contract is said to have been reached when all the players either do not Bid (or say 'Pass') or three consecutive players bid 'Pass' after any legal Bid.

- If your partner has made an opening bid, you will respond by a 'response bid', which will be described later.

- If you have checked your allotted cards for tricks and HCP (summation) and it is your 'turn' to make an opening call, then 'bid' your call or open the communication channel by describing your hand through a standard bidding system. The "Engineering System" is given below :

    Say 'Pass' if your cards in hand do not have a sum total of HCP and tricks as suggested below till your partner makes an opening bid.

- If you have a minimum of 13 HCP, five pictures and two and half tricks then you open by bidding "one Club". These are the three minimum, necessary and sufficient conditions to justify opening of a 'one Club' bid. Remember, one Club opening bid is an unlimited bid, which means you may have all thirteen pictures with 37 HCP and even then you will have to open one Club only. Since this one Club opening does not necessarily show the strength in a Club suit, this becomes an artificial opening bid.

- If you satisfy only two of the three necessary aforementioned conditions to bid 'one Club', then you should open a bid as follows:

    Bid '1 ♦' if you have five cards or more in one of the "Suits" (i.e. cards of same sign). Please note, this is also an artificial opening bid.

    Or

    Bid 'One No-trump' – if you do not have five cards or more in any one of the suits.

- Say 'pass' if your hand does not satisfy any of the conditions mentioned above.

- Now, you are ready to learn the responses to the opening calls.

So, come! Let's play and enjoy while you learn the responses.

Notes:

1. In general, if you have less than twelve HCP then you will not give an opening bid and will say 'pass'. However, you will respond to the opening call given by your partner, if any, when the biding turn comes back to you.

2. 'Unlimited bid' means you may have many more HCP and/or pictures and/or tricks than the necessary ones.

2.2   Engineering system : The First Responses

- When your partner has made an opening bid and it is your turn to bid, then respond as follows, provided the opponent (RHO) has bid a 'pass'; Unless your RHO bids a call intervening your bid, in that case the bids would be different than what is given below. This is explained in detail in the fifth chapter.

- First response to 'one Club' opening bid will be decided on the basis of your HCP and distribution of cards as described below. Please note, you must respond to one Club opening by your partner if your RHO has not intervened.

2.2.1 First response to one Club opening:

Sr.no.	Response	Meaning
a)	'One ♦'	0 to 7 HCP (or bad eight HCP) Any card distribution.
b)	'One No-trump'	9 to 11 HCP and an even distribution of hand i.e. no five cards in any of the 'suits'
c)	'One ♥'	8 to 11 HCP and five cards or more in any one of the suits.
d)	'Two ♣'	8 to 11 HCP and at least four cards in each of the 'major suits' i.e. Spades and Hearts.
e)	Level two bids in ♦s or ♥s or ♠s.	8 to 11 HCP and a "two suiter" hand. The "two suiter" hand means a hand with a minimum of ten cards in two suits. The suits may have a distribution of 5 - 5, 6 - 4 or 7 - 3. Bid the longer, i.e. a seven / six carder suit first, if two suits are 7 - 3 or 6 - 4, respectively. Bid the higher* suit if the cards are 5 - 5 (or even 6 - 5) in each suit. (Do not bid two Clubs even if it is longer or better of the two suits because it conveys different meaning. Choose one Heart bid, as suggested in 'c' above, in such a situation).
		* A higher suit means a suit higher in the hierarchy of suits, mentioned in 1.7.g.

f)	'One ♠'	With twelve or more HCP and any distribution of cards. Unlimited bid. It is also called a 'game force'. After this response the bidding will not stop till a minimum of any suitable game contract is reached by either partner.

It is better to start a bidding practice through exercises.

In the meantime, learn the responses to the opening calls of One Diamond and One No-trump, respectively.

I am sure it is interesting!

2.2.2 Engineering system : First response to one Diamond opening:

Sr.no.	Response	Meaning
a)	Pass	0 - 7 HCP with a five carder ♦ suit. As the opener has a limited weak opening bid, you may not lose a game and the opponents may intervene to allow the opener to bid his / her suit.
b)	1 ♥	0 - 11 HCP (high card points)
c)	1 ♠	12 HCP or more. Any distribution. A Game Force
d)	1 NT	9 to 11 HCP, normal distribution of cards 4-3-3-3- or 4-4-3-2
e)	2 ♣	8 to 11 HCP, and both major suits with a minimum of four cards in each major suit.

f)	2 ♦, 2 ♥, 2 ♠	Response bears the same meaning as indicated for one Club opening.
		Please remember that opener has a weak limited hand. Hence, it is better to respond by showing a "two suiter" hand only when both the suits have a minimum of five cards in each suit, which allosw you to bid higher suit first. However, if the "two suiter" hand has 6 - 4 distribution of suits, then, it is better to respond with one Heart and then chose an appropriate opportunity to show six carder suit.

2.2.3 Engineering system : First Response to an opening call of 'One No-trump'

Sr.no.	Response	Meaning
a)	Pass	0 to 11 HCP. Not interested in a bid. Not having any five carder suit. May bid a four carder suit with 8 to 11 HCP, if another turn comes to this responder in a competitive bidding.
b)	2 ♣	9 HCP or more – unlimited (like a "Stayman" convention). It is a forcing bid asking the opener, if he/she has a four carder major suit.

c)	2♦ / 2♥ / 2♠	6 to 8 HCP. Minimum of five cards in the bid suit. It is called as a "sign off" bid. Non-forcing. Ready to stop. May not be interested in bidding any further.
d)	2 NT	12 to 13 HCP. Normal distribution of cards. No five carder suit.
e)	3 NT	14 to 15 HCP. Normal distribution as stated in 'd)' above.
f)	3 ♣, 3 ♦, 3 ♥, 3 ♠	With 12 or more HCP. A minimum of five cards in a bid suit. Game forcing. Encouraging.

So come on! Carry out an exercise and enjoy as we learn further!

Engineering System
Opening Calls – Exercise No. 1

Assume you are a dealer. What will you bid with the following Hands?

[Spade (♠), Heart (♥), Diamond (♦), Club (♣)]

1. ♠-AK83, ♥-T52, ♦-J, ♣-KQJ93

2. ♠-5, ♥-K73, ♦-AQT9832, ♣-A6

3. ♠-Q974, ♥-QJ4, ♦-K65, ♣-852

4. ♠-JT62, ♥-A986, ♦-74, ♣-T74

5. ♠-864, ♥-AKT, ♦-KJ7, ♣-JT86

6. ♠-J73, ♥-643, ♦-A93, ♣-AQ93

7. ♠-AQ2, ♥-Q72, ♦-QT852, ♣-54

8. ♠-AQ2, ♥-KQ72, ♦-QT852, ♣-5

9. ♠-AQ2, H-KQ72, ♦-JT852, ♣-5

10. ♠-AQ2, ♥-KQ72, ♦-JT85, ♣-52

11. ♠-AQ2, ♥-KQ7, ♦-JT5, ♣-T987

12. ♠-JT7, ♥-KQ72, ♦-AJ, ♣-Q987

13. ♠-JT7, ♥-KQJ76, ♦-A, ♣-Q987

14. ♠-J7, ♥-AKQJ76, ♦-Q5, ♣-765

15. ♠-AK8, ♥-AKQJ7, ♦-AQ, ♣-KQJ

Having understood the opening calls and first round responses, let us carry out some exercise for a practice. Check your understanding and enjoy!

Engineering System
Opening Calls – Answers to Exercise No. 1

Sr. no.	Description	Bid
1	Three tricks, Six pictures, Fourteen HCP	One ♣
2	Three tricks, Four pictures, Thirteen HCP Diamond Suit	One ♦
3	Half trick, Four pictures, Eight HCP	Pass (No Bid)
4	One trick, Two pictures, Five HCP	No Bid (Pass)

5	Two & half tricks, Five pictures, Twelve HCP, No five card suit	I NT
6	Two & half tricks, Four pictures, Eleven HCP	No Bid
7	One & half trick, Four pictures, Eight HCP	No Bid
8	Two & half tricks, five pictures, Thirteen HCP	One ♣
9	Two & half tricks, five pictures, Twelve HCP One five card suit	One ♦
10	Two & half tricks, five pictures, Twelve HCP No five card suit	One NT
11	Two & half tricks, five pictures, Twelve HCP No five card suit	One NT
12	Two tricks, Six Pictures Thirteen HCP No Five card Suit	One NT
13	Two tricks, Six Pictures Thirteen HCP and a Five card Suit	One ♦
14	Two tricks, Six Pictures Thirteen HCP and a Five card Suit	One ♦
15	Six & half tricks, Eleven pictures, Twenty nine HCP	One ♣

Engineering System
Opening Calls – First Response, Exercise No. 2

How do you respond to the different opening calls of your partner as given below, when you have the followings cards with you (assume RHO is silent, i.e. bids pass) :-

[Spade (♠) Heart (♥), Diamond (♦), Club (♣)]

Assume the Opener has bid -

A) One ♣; or B) One ♦, or C) One No-trump. Chose appropriate responses for each of these opening calls if your hand is as stated below :

1. ♠-AK83, ♥-T52, ♦-J, ♣-KQJ93

2. ♠-52, ♥-K73, ♦-AQT983, ♣-A6

3. ♠-Q974, ♥-QJ4, ♦-K65, ♣-852

4. ♠-JT62, ♥-A986, ♦-74, ♣-T74

5. ♠-864, ♥-AKT, ♦-KJ7, ♣-JT86

6. ♠-J73, ♥-643, ♦-A93, ♣-AQ93

7. ♠-AQ2, ♥H-Q72, ♦-QT852, ♣-54

8. ♠-KT95, ♥-J985, ♦-64, ♣-K72

9. ♠-KT95, ♥-QJT9, ♦-64, ♣-K72,

10. ♠-KT95, ♥-AJT9, ♦-64, ♣-KQ2

11. ♠-KT985, ♥-AJT9, ♦-6, ♣-K72

12. ♠-K5, ♥-AJT9, ♦-64, ♣-KT872

13. ♠-53, ♥-AKJT, ♦-KQ6, ♣-Q872

14. ♠-T53, ♥-AKJ, ♦-KQ6, ♣-Q872

15. ♠-T9853, ♥-AX, ♦-Q653, ♣-82

16. ♠-K9853, ♥-A6543, ♦-Q8, ♣-2

❖ ❖ ❖

Engineering System
Opening Calls – First Response,
Answers to Exercise No. 2

A) First Response to opening call of one ♣ :

1	14 HCP, (Do not look at your ♣ suit)	1 ♠
2	13 HCP, (Do not look at your ♦ suit)	1 ♠
3	8 HCP, Poor cards with K or Q	1 ♦
4	5 HCP	1 ♦
5	12 HCP	1 ♠
6	11 HCP, No-trump distribution	1NT
7	10 HCP, One five card suit	1 ♥
8	7 HCP, Do not look at majors	1 ♦
9	9 HCP, Both Major suit four carder	2 ♣
10	13 HCP, Do not look at majors give game force	1 ♠
11	11 HCP, Indicate Both majors four carder	2 ♣
12	11 HCP, One five card suit	Bid 1 ♥
13	15 HCP, game force	1 ♠
14	15 HCP, game force	1 ♠
15	6 HCP, Over look 5 – 2 – 4 – 2 distribution, Reject	1 ♦
16	9 HCP, 5 – 5 – 2 – 1	2 ♠

B) Responses to Opening Call of One ♦ :

1	For 1, 2, 5, 10, 13 and 14 Respond	1 ♠
2	For 3, 4, 7, 8, 12 and 15 Respond	1 ♥
3	For 6	1 NT

4	For 9 and 11 Indicate Both Majors, Respond	2 ♣
5	For 16	2 ♠

C) Responses to 1 NT

1. The opener should know that you have a game in hand. It is important to make a game forcing response bid first. You are also worried about ♦ strength/ distribution. Respond with 3 ♣. This tells partner that you have a good five card ♣ holding with 12 plus HCP.

   If opener rebids 3 ♦ or 3 ♥, you rebid 3 ♠.

   If opener rebids 3 ♠ you may ask Aces by bidding 4 ♣/ 4 NT, as per your partnership understanding.

   Remember you have only a ♦ loser and your strong Club suit can cover up opener's losing ♥ cards.

   Answer to partners Ace asking call, if any, as per the convention on your 3 ♣ response.

2. You have a game forcing hand with a six carder suit. The quality of the ♦ suit is 'semisolid' as it has 'gaps' in the top five honor cards (i.e. Ace, King, Queen, Jack and Ten). Respond with 3♦.

   Keep quiet if the opener shuts with 3 NT

   You close bidding 3 NT, if the opener responds 3 ♥ or 3 ♠.

   Answer openers' Ace asking bid (4 ♣), if any, as per the convention.

3. You just have eight HCP. A perfectly balanced hand with 4 - 3 - 3 - 3 distribution and HCP evenly distributed. The opener is not likely to have more than sixteen HCP (All four Aces i.e. 16 HCP, four tricks but only four pictures).

Respond by a simple 'Pass'. You can avail an opportunity to bid your four carder Spade suit (by bidding 2 ♠) if the opponents intervene.

4. You have only five HCP. Although you have both majors, keep quiet unless your partner forces you to bid after the opponents intervene in the following manner:

Opener	RHO	You	LHO
I NT	P	P	Double
P	2 ♣	P	P
Double	P	Bid 2 ♥s & then Keep quiet	

5. You have exact twelve HCP. Balanced cards. No four carder major suit. Opener may have 12 to 16 HCP. You may lose a game if partner has 15 or 16 HCP. Hence bid 2 NT indicating 12 to 13 HCP with balanced distribution.

6. A peculiar hand. Eleven HCP and two Aces. Balanced cards. No four carder major suit. The quality of suits is also poor. Semi- solid honors. To bid 2 ♣s and then sign off in Two NT, if partner responds with 2 ♦, 2 ♥ or 2 ♠ could be one way to proceed. However, it is better to 'Pass' and watch your LHO's' bid. You are not losing a game unless your partner has sixteen HCP guarding both majors. A top hand your partner may have in such cases of bad luck is ♠ - KQ 10,

♥ - KQJX, ♦ - QJ10, ♣ - J10X. Otherwise in majority of the cases, opener is likely to have 12 to 14 HCP with poor control over one of the majors. Hence recommended response is 'No Bid'.

7. You have 10 HCP. Although quality of your five card ♦ suit is not good (it is not bad either), you should bid two ♣s and rebid three ♦s to show 10 - 11 HCP with five carder ♦ suit. Opener may pass three ♦s or return to 3 NT if he/she has the maximum HCP (15 – 16) and either top honors in ♦ or good control over other three suits.

   If the partner bids 2 NT over your 2 ♣, indicating maximum hand (15 - 16 HCP) you should rebid 3 NT to gamble a game bid, as your three ♦ bid would indicate 8 - 9 HCP only and a poor suit.

8. You have seven HCP. Both majors with four cards each. Quality of hand is poor. Do not overestimate majors, wait. Give No-Bid as first response. If LHO intervenes and the opener passes, watch the response of RHO. If RHO also passes you continue bidding as suggested :-

	Opener	RHO	You	LHO
Case I)	I NT	P	Pass	2 ♣ or 2 ♦ or 2 ♥
	P	P	Bid 2 ♥ or 2 ♠ (whichever is permissible)	
Case II)	I NT	P	Pass	Double

		2 ♣	Bid 2♥ or 2♠	
	Pass	or 2 ♦ or 2 ♥	(Whichever is permissible, otherwise pass)	

9. You have nine HCP. So together with the partner you have more HCP than the opponents. Your worry could be a Diamond suit.

   You must respond with a 2 ♣ and rebid 2 ♥ if the partner bids 2 ♦, or raise the level of major to three if the partner shows a four carder major. The partner may deny majors but show maximum HCP (15 - 16) by 2 NT, then you should pass with 8 - 9 HCP, or bid 3 NT with 10 - 11 HCP; it may be a good gamble.

10. You have 13 HCP, both major suits with four cards. Game must be bid. Your first response should be 2 ♣, if the opener responds a major, bid a game (4 level) in the same major. On your 2 ♣ response, if the partner rebids 2 NT indicating 15 - 16 HCP with no major suit, you should return to 3 NT Remember, 29 HCP are not enough for a small slam in No-trump. If the partner rebids 2 ♦, which is an indication of 12 -14 HCP without any major, then also you should return to 3 NT (game bid).

    Do not jump in a game bid, to begin with, which would assure your partner that you have 14 - 16 HCP with you. Opener may aspire for a slam if the opener has 15/16 HCP and suitable distribution (for instance, 4 - 4 - 3 - 2 or 4 - 4 - 4 - 1 with only one major).

11. Peculiar hand. Eleven HCP with both the major suits. It is not a game forcing hand unless the opener has a four carder major. Best way is to respond with two Clubs. If the partner rejects majors with a weak 2 ♦ response, then bid 2 ♠. If the partner rejects majors by a strong 2 NT, then bid a game in 4 ♠. If the opener shows any four carder major, then bid a game in that major suit.

12. You are just short of one HCP to a game forcing response. You have one major four carder and a minor five carder. Respond with 2 ♣, a forcing bid for opener. If opener rejects major by weak 2 ♦, rebid 3 ♣, which indicates five carder ♣ with just 10 - 11 HCP.

If the opener responds 2 ♠, which is a weak major (double ton) for you, you must return to 3 ♣ (your five card minor). Remember, the opener may have 12 to 16 HCP with 4 - 3 - 4 - 2 or 4 - 4 - 4 - 1 distribution. If the opener has both majors, he/she may return to 3 ♥ in which case you can jump to a 4 ♥ game bid. The opener may pass your 3 ♣ rebid if he/she has a weak hand (12 - 14 HCP) or can go to 3 NT with maximum (15 - 16) HCP.

13. You have fifteen HCP and one major four carder suit. Game is assured even with a minimum hand of the opener. There is a possibility of a small slam if the opener has 15 - 16 HCP and a suit fit.

You must respond 2 ♣, which is a one round forcing bid to the opener. If the opener rebids weak 2 ♦, you should jump to 3 NT.

If the opener rebids four carder major of your choice, (here 2 ♥s) you can ask Aces by 4 ♣ (Gerber convention) and stop at 4 ♥ if the opener has only one Ace, or if the partner shows two Aces; in that case, you ask Kings by 5 ♣ bid. You may stop at 5 ♥ if the opener has two Aces but one King only.

If the partner rebids a strong 2 NT you may plan to ask Aces/Kings by Gerber convention and stop at suitable level as discussed above.

If the partner rebids 2 ♠, just rebid a 3 NT game.

The opener may choose a strong 3 ♣ rebid to your 2 ♣s response, which would indicate 15 - 16 HCP, four carder ♣ and no four card major. You are free to use Gerber and reach a small slam in 6 ♣s if the number of Aces & Kings favours you.

14. You have 15 HCP. No four carder major. Just return to 3 NT in the first response as described in chapter 2.4.e

15. You have six HCP, a five card ♠ suit. Respond with a 2 ♠ even if RHO intervenes either by a double or any other bid at level two.

Your hand does not qualify for a game bid even if the opener rebids a strong (15 - 16 HCP) join by 3 ♠. It is recommended to bid 'pass' unless you have eight HCP and a longer ♠ suit.

In the cases where the responder is having a "two suiter" hand but less than 8 HCP, similar strategy should be used.

16. You have a "two suiter" hand with nine HCP. Bid
    2 ♣. If the partner rebids a major four carder, you
    can raise the level by one level, to show a minimum
    hand. The partner may bid a game if he /she has 15
    plus HCP.

    • If the partner responds with 2 ♦s then bid 2 ♥s to
      indicate 5 cards suit with 9-11 HCP.

    • If the partner responds with 2NT then bid, 3
      ♠ to show five cards with 9 HCP. In this case if
      partner returns to 3NT then bid 4 ♥s to show
      both (Majors) suits with five cards each.

BRIDGE PLAYERS

DO IT WITH FINESSE

Bidding And Reaching Contracts After First Round

While studying the objectives of a bidding system, it has been observed that you must reach a contract whichever is possible for you to make. If not, you should allow the opponents to settle with their contract. In this process, you may push opponents a little too further and defeat them, but while doing so, you should keep your contract within your own limits.

In section 1.7 r, HCP requirement in the combined hands for various goals (contracts) has been described. If your combined hands are not likely to have a game contract, then settle down at the lowest possible contract in competitive bridge or reach a par contract in rubber bridge.

There is a lower and upper level of HCP strength to each of the opening calls and responses. Part game or game zones are indicated by the responder assuming lowest HCP strength of the opener. In case the player opening a call and the responder, both have HCP at the maximum limit, then there is a possibility of making a game contract based on card distribution and control cards in shorter suits (especially in case of a No-trump contract).

The bidding cycle for an opening call and its first response is called first round, while in subsequent rounds of bidding, partners try to indicate the length of suits and distribution of cards. This section deals with how to describe your hand in the subsequent rounds and how to reach the appropriate contracts.

3.2   Bidding after opening 'One ♣':

Opening 1 ♣ and its responses have been described in the earlier chapter.

3.2.1   Assume you have opened 1♣ and you have received a response of 1 ♦ from your partner, then bid as follows (also assume that the opponents are silent, i.e. they bid pass only) :

e.g.

	You	Partner	Explanation of the bid
a)	1 ♣	1 ♦	
	1 ♥		The opener indicates five carder Heart with 13 -18 HCP.
b)	1 ♣	1 ♦	
	2 ♣		Indicates five carder Club 13 -18 HCP.
c)	1 ♣	1 ♦	

	2 ♦		Here a pass or no bid by the opener would have indicated 13 to 15 HCP and a five carder ♦. However, 2 ♦ will indicate a five carder Diamond and more i.e. 16-20 HCP.
d)	1 ♣	1 ♦	
	1NT		This will indicate 13 -18 HCP balanced hand, no five carder suit.
e)	1 ♣	1 ♦	
	2 ♥/ 2 ♠		18 to 20 HCP. A five carder bid suit (♥ or ♠).. If the partner has at least 3 carder join with four HCP or more, then it is possible to have a game contract.

Note : In case the opener has 18 - 20 HCP but a five carder minor suit (Club or Diamond), it cannot fetch a minor game unless the responder has a good join with eight HCP.

	Opener	Responder	
f)	1 ♣	1 ♦	
	2NT		This indicates 20 - 22 HCP, all suits guarded by at least one control.
g)	1 ♣	1 ♦	
	3NT		Indicating 23 - 24 HCP, all suits guarded by at least one control.

Note: The meaning of at least one control, for No-trump bids, is at least a singleton Ace or doubleton King or triple ton QJ combination.

Therefore, if the responder has a six carder suit and 6 - 8 HCP, then he/she should assess the possibility of a slam (by Ace asking etc.) in the cases of (f) and (g).

h)	1 ♣	1 ♦	
	4 ♣		Should be considered and responded to as an Ace asking bid by the responder.
i)	1 ♣	1 ♦	
	3 ♣ or 3 ♦		The opener has 18 plus HCP with a five card minor suit. These are all game forcing bids. The responder may pass with 0 - 3 HCP. If the responder joins the bid suit with triple-ton or a doubleton honor and has 6 - 8 HCP, then the responder should raise the level of bid suit by one if the hand is unbalanced, or bid 3 NT if the hand has a balanced distribution.

j)	1 ♣	1 ♦	
	3 ♥ or 3 ♠		The opener has 18 plus HCP with at least a five carder major suit. These are game forcing bids. The responder may pass with 0 - 3 HCP. If the responder joins the bid suit with a triple-ton or a doubleton honor and has 4 - 8 HCP, then the responder should raise the level to a game contract or even assess a Slam if he/she has a good join and a long side suit with 7 - 8 HCP.

3.2.2 A response of 1 ♥ to a one Club opening indicates (a part game zone) 8 - 11 HCP with some five carder suit with the responder. Therefore, it is better for the opener to allow the responder to indicate his/her five carder suit at the lowest level. This could be simply done by giving a 1NT response by the opener. The 1NT bid by the opener, should not be interpreted as a balanced hand by the responder, i.e. no five carder suit with the opener. However, any suit bid in the subsequent rounds by the opener should be interpreted as a four carder suit only, e.g.:

	Opener	Responder	Explanation of the bid
a)	1 ♣	1 ♥	
	1 ♠		The opener has a five carder Spade suit with 13-16 HCP.
b)	1 ♣	1 ♥	
	1NT		Forcing bid, asking partner to show the five carder suit. Opener may or may not be having a five carder suit and may also have high HCP.
c)	1 ♣	1 ♥	
	1NT	2 ♦	Five carder Diamond suit with the responder.
	2NT		This will indicate 16 - 18 HCP with the opener and an invitation to bid 3NT (game) if the responder has the maximum HCP range. ♦ support could be a singleton or doubleton with the opener. If the responder has any other four carder suit, one should bid that with 10-11 HCP. The responder should pass with minimum HCP and poor ♦ suit or should signoff in ♦ (3 ♦) if the ♦ suit is good but has a minimum hand (8 - 9).
			The responder should bid 3 NT with 10-11 HCP and no other four carder suit.

Note: With the one NT rebid by the opener, the count strength of the opener is not revealed. His/her strength and distribution could be indicated in the subsequent rounds after the responder indicates his/her five carder suit, as shown in the examples above.

d)	1 ♣	1 ♥	
	2 ♣ / 2 ♦ / 2 ♥		The opener has a five carder bid suit. 13 - 16 HCP.

e)	1 ♣	1 ♥	
	1 ♠ (Spade suit)	2 ♥ (Heart Suit)	A five carder ♥ suit. Please note if the responder, interestingly, responds here with 1 NT then it is only to indicate a singleton or void in the opener's ♠ suit showing 5–4–4–0 or 5–4–3–1 distribution.
	3 ♥		This indicates that the opener has a 3 card ♥ join but has a minimum hand, i.e. 13-15 HCP and expects the responder to bid a game only if he/she has 10-11 HCP.

3.2.3 Bidding after a No-trump response to 1 ♣ opening call

If a responder calls 1NT to 1 ♣ opening call, it means 9 - 11 HCP and a balanced hand, i.e. distribution of suits is 4 - 3 - 3 - 3 or 4 - 4 - 3 - 2. In the exceptional circumstances, the responder may have one of the major suits with singleton and all other four card suits (4 - 1 - 4 - 4 distribution, as he/she has not responded with a 2 ♣ major showing bid).

In such cases the opener should bid a natural five carder suit bid in the second round; or he/she could choose from the various other options depending upon HCP strength and cards distribution, as shown in the examples below:

	Opener	Responder
a)	1 ♣	INT
	2 ♣	It is a forcing and unlimited bid. The responder should treat this bid as a "Stayman" and show a four carder major, if any. If the opener, in subsequent round, rebids 3 ♣ then he/she has a five card ♣ suit and is a sign off. The responder has to keep quiet. If, on 2 ♣, the responder shows a four carder major and if the opener rebids it at level three, then the opener has a minimum hand but with four cards in the bid major and expects the responder to bid the a game only if the responder has the maximum hand (10 - 11 HCP).
		For example -

b)	1 ♣	1NT
	2 ♣	2 ♥ (Minimum four carder ♥)
	3 ♥	The opener joins the suit with four cards but has 13 - 14 HCP. It is up to the responder to decide whether to pass (weak 8 - 9 HCP) or to bid a game, i.e. 4 ♥ with 10 - 11 HCP.
c)	1 ♣	1NT
	2 ♣	2 ♥ (Minimum four carder ♥)
	4 ♥	The opener is happy to bid a game.
d)	1 ♣	1NT
	2 ♣	2 ♥ (Minimum four carder ♥)
	2NT	No four carder ♥, but the opener has 15 - 17 HCP. Invitation to the responder to bid a 3 NT game if he/she has 10 - 11 HCP (Maximum range).
e)	1 ♣	1NT
	2 ♣	2 ♦/2 ♥/ or 2 ♠
	Pass	The opener has a minimum hand (13 - 14 HCP) with a three carder responder's bid suit. The opener does not see a game.
f)	1 ♣	1NT
	2 ♦ or 2 ♥ or 2 ♠	It is a sign off. A five card bid suit with 13 - 15 HCP. The responder may raise the level of bid suit by one, if he/she has the maximum hand i.e. 10 - 11 HCP and good supporting cards which will be treated as an invitation for the opener to bid a game if he/she has a good quality of hand.

g)	1 ♣	1NT
	2NT	The opener has 15 - 17 HCP and a balanced distribution. It is an invitation to the responder to bid 3NT (game) if he/she has the maximum HCP range (i.e. 10-11)
h)	1 ♣	1NT
	3 ♣, 3 ♦, 3 ♥, 3 ♠	Game force. 16 - 18 HCP, 5 carder bid suit. Asking partner to bid a game either in 3 NT or join the opener's major bid suit with 3 cards in 4 ♥ or 4 ♠.
i)	1 ♣	1NT
	3NT	Game bid. Sign off.
j)	1 ♣	1NT
	4 ♣	Forcing, Ace asking bid. The opener is interested in a slam bid depending on Aces (and or Kings - if asked subsequently by 5 ♣ bid).

As 1 ♣ is an unlimited opening call, on partners response of 1NT, it is only the opener who can judge whether it is a game or a part game with them, as the responder has already indicated the count strength and card distribution to the opener, and therefore the opener should clarify the situation to the responder in the next immediate subsequent round (rounds) as described above.

3.2.4 On 1 ♣ opening, if the responder indicates 8 - 11 HCP and both major suits with a minimum of 4 cards each, by bidding 2 ♣ response (a major showing bid), then the opener should decide whether the partnership has a part game, likely game, sure game or likely (or sure) slam. Watch the bidding in subsequent rounds.

	Opener	Responder
a)	1 ♣	2 ♣ (8-11 HCP, both majors)
	2 ♥ or 2 ♠	Four carder major, with a minimum hand i.e. 13 - 14 HCP The responder has to bid a game, if he/she has a maximum hand, i.e. 10 - 11 HCP. The responder may bid the other major suit if it is a five carder and also has a maximum hand, which is game forcing in either of the suits of the opener's choice.
b)	1 ♣	2 ♣
	2 ♥	2 ♠ (Responder shows 5 carder ♠ suit, 4 carder ♥ suit and is a game going hand, i.e. 10-11 HCP)
c)	1 ♣	2 ♣
	2 ♠	3 ♥ (5 carder ♥ & 4 carder ♠. Game forcing). The opener should bid a major game either in ♥ (if joining ♥ with good 3 cards) or in ♠, as per his/her choice.
d)	On a 1 ♣ opening if the responder indicates 8 - 11 HCP with both majors, the opener should give four carder major at level threes to force a game, i.e. with 15 - 16 HCP.	
	1 ♣	2 ♣

	3 ♥ or 3 ♠	This indicates a minimum of 15 - 16 HCP. It is a game forcing bid. The responder may bid a major game in the agreed major or may choose a change of suit (e.g. 4 ♦, without crossing the game level of the agreed major suit) which indicates at least 5 cards in ♦, and will always reach at least a game.
e)	1 ♣	2 ♣ (8 - 11 HCP, Both majors)
	4 ♣	Ace asking. The opener has a very strong hand, and is happy to know that the responder has both majors. The responder should keep on supplying the information about his/her hand, as may be asked by the opener using Ace and or King asking bids. The final contract is to be decided by the opener.
f)	1 ♣	2 ♣
	2 ♥	3 ♣ or 3 ♦. This indicates a four or five carder bid minor suit, in addition to both majors with 4 cards of each. So the responder may have 4–4–5–0 or 4–4–4–1 distribution. The count range remains unaffected, i.e. 8 - 11.
g)	1 ♣	2 ♣ 8 - 11 HCP, Both Majors

	2 ♦	This indicates no four carder major suit and minimum (13 - 15 HCp) hand with the opener.
		The responder may bid a five card major, with (8-9 HCP) minimum hand at 2 level.
		The responder should bid 2 ♥ even with four cards in ♥ but singleton / void in ♦ suit, of his/her hand is a minimum hand (8 - 9 HCP).
		The responder to bid his/her five cards mojor suit, with maximum hand (10 - 11 HCP) at three level.
		The responder can pass with atleast a trippleton ♦ suit and minimum hand (8 - 9 HCP).
		The responder to bid 2NT with maximum hand (10 - 11 HCP) and no-five carder major.
		The responder should bid four or five carder ♣ or ♦ suit with (10 - 11 HCP) maximum hand.
		i. e. 4-4-1-4 distribution or 4-4-5-0 distribution.
h)	1 ♣	2 ♣

	2NT	This indicates that the opener has no four carder major suit but has a maximum hand (16 - 18 HCP). Game forcing. The responder should bid a five carder major suit at three level, is any The responder should bid 3 ♣ ro 3 ♦ if he/she has 4 or 5 cards in that suit, in addition to both majors. i.e. the cards are 4-4-4-1 or 4-4-5-0. The responder should pass with bad 8 counts and poor suits. The responder should bid 3NT if has (10 - 11 HCP) maximum hand.
i)	1 ♣	2 ♣
	4 ♣	This is an Ace asking bid. Opener is very happy that responder has minimum 4 cards in each majar with 8 -11 HCP. Opener may have 18 + HCP.

3.2.5 If the responder has a "two suiter" hand (minimum ten cards in two suits) with 8 - 11 HCP, then he/she should first respond with a longer* suit or higher** of the two five card suits and then he/she may rebid the other suit if the opener continues the enquiry.

* Longer suit means six carder if the suits are 6 - 4 distribution. The longer suit may sometimes have 7 cards while the other suit will have only 3 cards, which

would be indicated by an immediate rebid of the longer suit.

** Higher suit means higher in the hierarchy of suits. If the suits are 6 - 5 distribution, then also bid the higher suit first. If the suits have 7 - 3 distribution, then bid the longer suit first and re-bid it on the next turn. e.g.:

	Opener	Responder	Meaning of the bid
a)	1 ♣	2 ♦ or 2 ♥ or 2 ♠ or 3 ♣	• The bid suit is either a longer (a minimum of six cards or more with the other suit, if the bid later has four cards only), or higher of the two suits which have a minimum of five cards each. (ref. 2.2.e) • A 'two' suiter response • 8 - 11 HCP

b) Let us take an example of a response of a "two suiter" hand –

Opener   Responder

1 ♣   2 ♥

(i)   The opener always has an option of passing the responder's 'two suiter' response bid, if he/she has a minimum hand, 13 - 14 HCP and a poor quality of hand, with all HCPs in Kings and Jacks like unsupported honors etc. and may be with poor supporting cards in the responders' suit.

(ii)   The opener may show his/her five card suit, if not joining the responder's suit and has minimum HCP, i.e. 13 - 14 HCP. The responder then may rebid opener's suit with three card support and 10 - 11 HCP or show the second five card suit also if has 10 - 11 HCP. The responder may rebid the same suit if it is a seven carder one and has 10 - 11 HCP.

(iii)   The opener may bid a game (4 ♥) if he/she has a minimum of 3 cards of ♥ with 15 - 16 HCP.

(iv)   The opener may ask Aces by 4 ♣ bid, if he/she has a good ♥ support but 18 plus HCP, to estimate a slam.

(v)   The opener may bid 2NT, forcing the responder to show the second suit (even if it is a four carder one) and then decide the final contract. The opener must have 16 plus HCP range and might be planning to go to 3NT

Opener	Responder
c) 1 ♣	2 ♥ – 'two suiter', ♥ is longer or higher of the two five carder suits.
2 ♠ A Five card Suit	3 ♦ - Since the opener has not changed the level (level two) of bidding, the responder is taking opportunity

| 13 - 14 HCP | to show the second suit, ♦ suit could be four or five carder, hand is 10 - 11 HCP. Non forcing. |

3 ♥ The opener cannot play in 3 ♦. A minimum hand. ♥ is at least doubleton. Non-forcing.

In such cases if the opener has a strong six card suit, headed by KQJ, then he/she may rebid 3 ♠ instead of 3 ♥. The opener may bid a game in ♠s or ♥s depending on the quality of cards and when all HCP are concentrated in the useful suits.

3.2.6 If the opener has opened 1 ♣ and the responder has 12 HCP or more,

balanced or unbalanced (even a 'two suiter') hand, then it is the duty of the responder to first give a game forcing bid of 1 ♠, so that the bidding continues till at least a suitable game contract is reached.

	Opener	Responder	
a)	1 ♣	1 ♠	Game force. The subsequent bids would indicate the suits and final contract will never be less than a game contract.

The opener may rebid to 1 ♠ response either by a five card suit bid e.g. 2 ♦, 2 ♥, 2 ♠ or bid 1NT to indicate no five carder suit or may also give a rebid of 2 ♣ to which responder must show a four carder major, as if it is an asking bid like "Stayman".

e.g.

b) 1 ♣   1 ♠

   2 ♦, 2 ♥ or 2 ♠ _ This bid indicates a five carder bid
                      suit with the opener. Could be a
                      minimum hand (13 - 15 HCP)

                      The responder may indicate a
                      three carder join or indicate his/
                      her own five carder suit.

                      Jumps are not advised by the opener
                      even with high count strength.

Or

c) 1 ♣   1 ♠

   2 ♣   _   It should be treated as an asking a
                        four carder major.

                        A rebid of 3 ♣ by the opener, later
                        on, will indicate a 5 carder Club
                        suit. and a minimum hand.

                        If the responder has a five carder
                        major, while responding to a
                        "Stayman", it is advisable to rebid
                        that major in subsequent round to
                        indicate five cards.

e.g.

d) 1 ♣   1 ♠

   2 ♣   2 ♥ – Minimum four carder ♥

   2NT or 3 ♣   3 ♥ – Minimum five carder ♥

(13 – 15 HCP)

Here 2NT rebid by the opener indicates no four carder ♥ and the possibility of having a four carder ♠ while the 3 ♣ rebid indicates a five carder Club, and also clarifies that earlier bid of 2 ♣ was not necessarily a "Stayman".

e) 1 ♣   1 ♠

    1NT   ___ This may be a limited or minimum 1 ♣ opening with 13 - 15 HCP and has no five card suit.

                             This hand could be 4–3–3–3 or 4–4–3–2 and probably not having a four carder major, as a four carder single major would also invite the bid of a 2 ♣ response. This call could also be a waiting bid with a very strong hand, waiting to know, if the responder has any five carder suit.

In case of 3.2.5 (e), if the responder has 12 - 14 HCP and a balanced distribution of cards, then on 1NT rebid by the opener, responder should simply shut the bid by 3NT. However, if the responder has 15 or more HCP and no five carder suit it is advisable to give a forcing "Stayman" of 2 ♣. e.g.

	Opener	Responder	Meaning of the bid
f)	1 ♣	1 ♠	

	1NT	2 ♣	Forcing. To be treated as a "Stayman" and opener should respond with a four carder suit. A subsequent rebid of 3 ♣ would indicate a five card Club suit with the responder.
g)	1 ♣	1 ♠	
	1NT	2 ♣	Treat it as a forcing "Stayman".
	2 ♦ or 2 ♥ or 2 ♠ or) 3 ♣ or 2NT)		A four carder suit bid. Respond strictly as described in 3.4.4 later. Do not stop belows a game bid.

h) The opener may have a strong hand (16 or more HCP) but he/she may not have a five card suit then on 1 ♠ response opener should rebid 2NT.

	Opener	Responder	Meaning of the bid
	1 ♣	1 ♠	
	2NT		(16 – 18 HCP, no singleton, control in all suits). This indicates a slam if 1 ♠ responder has 14 HCP or more. In such a case responder should bid a slam in his/her five carder suit or in NT.

i) If the opener has 18 or more HCP, on 1 ♠ response, a small slam is a possibility in the least. However, there is no need to jump in levels while bidding. You can describe lengths of suits to each other to understand whether trump suit is useful or No-trump should be the final contract. Use Ace asking (4 ♣) and also King asking (5 ♣) convention for investigation. However, if ♣ is going to be agreed trump suit you can always use 4 NT as Ace asking and 5 NT as King asking bid.

3.3   Bidding after 1 ♦ opening call :

Opening 1 ♦ means you are satisfying only two out of three conditions for opening with 1 ♣. However, you also have some suit with five cards. So it is a weak opening with 12 to 16 HCP.

The responder, in general, bids a negation with 0 - 11 HCP. However, the responder knows that the opener has a weak hand and may chose to pass or give no bid if the responder has 0 - 6 HCP and a five card ♦ suit.

	Opener	Responder	Meaning of the bid
a)	1 ♦	1 ♥	Negation. 0 - 11 HCP. Part game zone.

If the opener passes this negation, it would mean that the opener has 12 to 13 HCP and a poor five carder ♥ suit. The opener should rebid 2 ♥ if he/she has a five card ♥ suit with 14 – 16 HCP, or has unbalanced hand like 5–4–3–1 or 5–4–2–2.

	Opener	Responder	
b)	1 ♦	1 ♥	
	1 ♠ or 2 ♣ or 2 ♦		This indicates a five carder bid suit.

With all the above rebids by the opener (except 'Pass'), the responder can either i) Pass or ii) raise the level of opener's suit or iii) change of suit and bid a new five carder suit or iv) bid a no-trump in the following situations.

3.3.1

(i) If the responder has less than six HCP, then he/she may pass the rebid of the opener even if he/she has a singleton/doubleton in the opener's suit. The responder may bid a new five or four carder suit at the same level if he/she has a void, in opener's suit.

(ii) The responder should raise the level by one if the opener has rebid a five card major suit and responder has 8 - 11 HCP and a minimum three cards in openers' rebid suit. If the opener has rebid a five card minor, then the responder should only raise its level by one, if the responder joins with minimum 3 cards and has 10 – 11 HCP, e.g.

	Opener	Responder	
c)	1 ♦	1 ♥	
	2 ♥ (Five carder ♥ with 14 – 16 HCP)	4 ♥	A game bid. 10 – 11 HCP, Minimum 3 carder ♥

	Opener	Responder
d)	1 ♦	1 ♥
	1 ♠ (Spade suit)	2 ♠ joining Spade suit. 8 - 9 HCP.

Here the opener can chose to bid a game in 4 ♠ if has 15 - 16 HCP. The responder should bid 3 ♠ instead of 2 ♠ if he/she has 10 - 11 HCP and a good ♠ support.

	Opener	Responder
e)	1 ♦	1 ♥
	2 ♣ (or 2 ♦)	3 ♣ (or 3 ♦) (a minimum of 3 card support in opener's suit and 10 - 11 HCP)

If the opener has 16 HCP and a good control cards in all the suits, then he/she may think of a game in 3NT.

(iii) The responder may think of bidding a five carder major suit if he/she has a void / singleton in the openers' suit without changing the level, provided the responder has a long major suit or has 10 - 11 HCP, e.g. :-

	Opener	Responder
f)	1 ♦	1 ♥
	1 ♠	Responder should pass at this level even if he/she has a void or singleton in ♠ and a weak hand. Should bid six carder suit with 4 plus HCP and must bid a new five card suit, with 8 plus HCP if void / singleton in the opener's suit.
		If the responder has passed the Hand in the above situations and gets another opportunity to bid freely, then he/she should bid a five card suit to save partner even with low HCP.

	Opener	Responder
g)	1 ♦	1 ♥
	2 ♣	2 ♥ (Minimum five card suit, 10 - 11 HCP)

The responder at times may chose to bid 2NT as follows.

	Opener	Responder	Meaning of the bid
h)	1 ♦	1 ♥	
	2 ♥	2Nt	• 10 - 11 HCP • One Stopper in ♠. • Double ton ♥. • A long good quality minor suit. • Gamble bid to reach 3NT game. • Ready to play 3 ♥.

The 2NT response allows the opener to think of a 3NT game if he/she has 15 - 16 HCP and a solid bid suit or long bid suit.

3.3.2 Responding 1NT to 1 ♦ opening:-

1NT is a natural response to 1 ♦ if responder has 9 - 11 HCP and balanced/No-trump distribution. The opener will show a five carder suit if he/she has a good quality of suit but weak opening (or may pass weak hand with poor suit like 10, 8, 7, 5, 2.

The opener may have 14 - 16 HCP and 5–4–3–1 distribution.

In such cases the opener rebids five carder suits and on an opportunity in subsequent round may bid the four card suit.

e.g. :-

	Opener	Responder
a)	1 ♦	1NT
	2 ♣ or 2 ♦ or 2 ♥ or 2 ♠	• It is a five carder bid suit • Non forcing. • Responder should raise by one level if joins with 3 card and 10 - 11 HCP. • Responder may show new four carder suit at same level if has 10 - 11 HCP but doubleton in openers bid suit. • Responder may jump to a game bid if the opener has bid a five card major suit (♥ or ♠) provided that the responder has a good join (a double-ton honor or a minimum of triple ton support) and 10 - 11 HCP.

b)	1 ♦	1NT
	3 ♣ or 3 ♦ or 3 ♥ or 3 ♠	• Non forcing bid • Indicates semi-solid six card suit. • 15 – 16 HCP range. • Ready to play 3NT if the responder has 10 – 11 HCP. • Ready to play in a major game 4 ♥ - 4 ♠ if the opener has rebid a major at 3 level and the responder bids a game (provided the responder has a good support with 10 - 11 HCP).
c)	1 ♦	1NT
	3NT	• Shut bid. • It is often a gamble bid • May have long solid/semi-solid suit to quickly collect tricks. • Assumes partners supporting cards in the opener's hidden long suit. • Assumes 10 - 11 HCP with the responder and at least contribution of 2 or 3 tricks.

The partnership has a lot of scope to design variations after a 1 ♦

opening and 1NT responses. Practice may lead to such variations.

3.3.3 Many a times 1 ♦ opener has a four card major suit along with a five carder suit. Since a major suit game (4 ♥ or 4 ♠) requires lesser tricks to be made and hence less count strength than a minor suit game, investigating such a game plays a very important role.

This system provides instant information of having both major suits with the responder, each having at least four cards with 8 - 11 HCP using 2 ♣ response.

For e.g.

	Opener	Responder	Meaning of the bid
a)	1 ♦	2 ♣	• 8 - 11 HCP • Both major suits with at least 4 cards each. • Distribution of suits could be 5–4–4–0, 5–4–3–1, 4–4–4–1 or 4–4–3–2

i) Here the opener may bid a four carder major at level two (2 ♥ or 2 ♠) if his/her hand is weak or jump to 4 carder major at level three (3 ♥ or 3 ♠) if hand is strong, i.e. with 15 - 16 HCP.

ii) However, if the opener does not have a four carder major and has a five card minor, then he/she should bid the five card suit i.e. 2 ♦ or 3 ♣.

iii) Lastly if the opener has both minors 5–4 and has no major but has 15 - 16 HCP then he/she may bid 2NT to invite the responder to bid a game in 3NT with maximum HCP (10 - 11).

3.3.4 Game forcing response: 1 ♠

In this system the 1 ♠ response even to a 1 ♦ opening indicates 12 plus HCP and is taken as a game force. Since 1 ♦ itself is a limited opening bid (12 - 16 HCP), it is the duty of the responder to investigate the appropriate game contract.

The natural way for the opener is to indicate a five carder suit on 1 ♠ response and show a four carder suit, if any, in subsequent rounds to describe the hand to the game forcing responder.

	Opener	Responder
e.g. a)	1 ♦	1 ♠ game force
	2 ♦ – five card suit	2 ♥ five carder Heart
	2 ♠ – No. 3 carder ♥	
	But has 4 cards in	
	♠ along with	
	5 cards in ♦.	
Or b)	1 ♦	1 ♠
	2 ♣ – five card suit	2 ♠ five card suit
	3 ♦ – No. 3 carder ♠	
	But has 4 cards in ♦.	
	Non forcing.	
c)	1 ♦	1 ♠
	2 ♣ Or 2 ♦ or 2 ♥ or	2NT – Indicates 14 - 16
	2 ♠ (a five card	HCP range. Invitation to
	bid suit)	play 3NT game.
d)	1 ♦	1 ♠
	2 ♣ or 2 ♦ or 2 ♥	Rebid of the opener's
	or 2 ♠ (A five carder	suit at level 3 indicates a
	suit bid)	minimum of three
		carder support,
		12 - 14 HCP.
		Ready to play 3NT or
		a game in the major
		suit bid of the opener.

	Opener	Responder
e)	1 ♦	1 ♠
	3 ♣ or 3 ♦ or	Responder to take a

3 ♥ or 3 ♠ Indicates minimum 5 Card or longer bid suit and Unbalanced distribution, with 15 - 16 HCP.

decision whether to bid a Game or Slam on the basis of supporting cards to opener's bid suit in the his / her hand and the HCP strength.

3.3.5 'two suiter' response –

If the responder has a "two suiter" hand with 8 - 11 HCP the responses and subsequent bidding will be similar to such responses with 1 ♣ opening, e.g.

	Opener	Responder
a)	1 ♦	2 ♦ - 8 - 11 HCP

Longer or higher of two five carder suits.
(barring a Club suit)

2 ♥ Relay to continue

b)   1 ♦   2 ♠

2NT Relay to continue

Remember, 1 ♦ opener has a five card suit with a limited 12 - 16 HCP. While responding with "two suiter' hands, be careful not to cross the limits of level three or you may land into difficulty. It is better to respond with 1 ♥ if you have a "two suiter' hand with minor suits or a poor count range. It is also better to respond with a "two suiter' hand only if the responder has a minimum of five cards in each suit.

If the responder has a 'two suiter' hand with 12 or more HCP then the response must be a game forcing '1 ♠' only.

3.4 Opening One No-trump: Responses and Subsequent Bidding

3.4.1 It has been discussed about opening a 1NT and its responses in earlier chapters.

Bidding and playing without any trump suit has always been a challenging situation. Based on the partner's responses the opener has to often decide whether to 'pass' or bid any further.

e.g.   Opener   Responder

  a) 1NT   2 ♦ or 2 ♥ or 2 ♠

                            It is a simple weak response Indicating five card bid suit with 6 - 8 HCP range.

Generally the opener is supposed to pass this response, if he/she has 12 - 14 HCP. In unfortunate situations the opener may be forced to open 1NT with 4–4–4–1 distribution and the responder may bid his/her singleton suit. It is better for the opener to pass this bid, with weak hands, with or without intervention. The responder may chose to bid other four carder suit after intervention or may rebid six card suit after intervention. If the opener is weak (12 - 14 HCP) he/she must pass the hand.

In case, in the above situation, the opener has 15 - 16 HCP with a singleton/doubleton in the responder's suit, he/she may choose to bid next higher four carder suit inviting the partner to pass or bid another four card suit. e.g.:

	Opener	Responder
b)	1NT	2 ♦
	2 ♥ (No ♦ support	2 ♠ or 3 ♣
	But has a four carder	Not ready to play in 2♥.
	♥ & 15 – 16 HCP,	Has a four carder
		bid suit.
	4 – 4 – 4 – 1 or	Please note,
	4 – 4 – 3 – 2	the responder
		Distribution)
		may rebid 3 ♦ suit
		which is possible.

	Opener	Responder
c)	1NT	2 ♥ or 2 ♠
	3 ♥ or 3 ♠	

Rebid of the responder's major suit
at 3 level if he/she has a four carder join
With 15 - 16 HCP. Invitation to game.

3.4.2 Remember, the responder may give an invitation
to a game by i) 2NT or ii) 3 ♣, 3 ♦, 3 ♥ or 3 ♠
bid.

These proposals to bid a game are not possible only
if the opener is very weak with 12 - 13 HCP and/or a
poor quality of hand with a weak or no 3 carder support.

e.g. :	Opener	Responder
a)	1NT	2NT (12 - 13 HCP)
	3NT (15 - 16 HCP)	The responder must
		pass instead of giving
		2NT if he/she does
		not have 12 HCP.
b)	1NT	3 ♣ or 3 ♦

		Minimum of five cards in bid suit. 12 - 13 HCP.

3NT
(15 - 16 HCP even if the
 Opener has three supporting
Cards in the responder's minor suit.
A cheaper game.)

c)   1NT

3 ♥ or 3 ♠
5 carder bid suit.
12 - 13 HCP.

3NT	The responder here
(14 - 16 HCP,	has a choice to
protecting the other	bid a major suit game
major suit like QJT9 etc.	if his / her HCPs are
A doubleton join	concentrated in the
in the responder's suit.)	bid suit and or has a
	longer suit.

Opener	**Responder**
d) 1NT	3 ♥ or 3 ♠
	(as above)

4 ♥ or 4 ♠
Bid a major game in
Responders' suit if you
have a good supporting cards
in the bid suit, i.e. minimum
3 carder support.

3.4.3 On 1NT opening the responder may chose to bid directly a game in major suits, if he/she has a longer or stronger hand of 13 - 14 HCP, and a solid major suit with 5 to 6 cards.

3.4.4 A 2 ♣ response to 1NT opening is always a forcing bid. The opener must respond with a four carder major. It is treated as a "Stayman" convention. A 2 ♦ rebid by the opener would indicate 12 - 14 HCP and no four card major.

	Opener	Responder
a)	1 NT	2 ♣
	2 ♦	2 ♥ or 2 ♠
	No major four cards	This 2 ♥ or 2 ♠
	Weak 12 - 14 HCP.	bid by responder
		indicates a five card bid
		suit with 9 - 11 HCP.

b)	1NT	2 ♣
	2 ♥ or 2 ♠	3 ♣ or 3 ♦
		Indicates a good five card suit and 9 - 11 HCP, with four cards in other unbid major suit. Not forcing but invitation to 3NT for the opener if he/she has 15 - 16 HCP.

	Opener	Responder
c)	1NT	2 ♣
	2NT	
	(shows 15 - 16 HCP	
	ready to play 3NT if	
	the responder has 10+ HCP	

d)   1NT   2 ♣
     3 ♣
     (No major four carder,
     Four carder ♣ and
     15 - 16 HCP).

In cases of (c) and (d) above, if the responder rebids a five carder suit, he/she is forcing to a game either in the bid suit (if major), provided the opener has a triple-ton support or in the No-trump. The opener cannot 'pass' this hand and must bid appropriate game contract.

It is obvious that for a 1NT opening, the 2 ♣ response keeps the bidding alive and the responder only has a choice to decide whether to go for a game or a slam contract. The responder may use 4 ♣ bid or 4NT bid to ask Aces depending upon the agreed suit, to avoid confusion.

However, a responder is free to pass anytime during the bidding at the appropriate level even when he/she has used a '2 ♣' forcing response.

3.4.5 'Two suiter' responses

On a 1NT opening if the responder has a 'two suiter' hand, it is difficult to express it to the opener. The entire decision making process rests with the responder to choose a proper route for estimating a game or a part game zone.

a)   If the responder is weak i.e. less than six HCP then he/she should sign off in the longer suit (provided it is not a Club suit).

If the responder is weak but has six carder Club he/she should 'pass' and wait for the intervention, if any. If doubled by the opponents, then bid a longer suit (even if it is a Club suit) immediately, with or without a 'two suiter' hand, e.g.

Opener	RHO	Responder
1NT	Double	2 ♣ - This should not be treated as a "Stayman" by the partner. It is a weak five card ♣ suit.

(with such a typical intervention, the responder can choose several options if he/she is strong. This is separately dealt with in the subsequent chapters).

b) If the responder is strong, then he/she can choose to give a jump bid in a longer suit as described above or if he/she has major suits as one of the two suits, then he/she can choose a 2 ♣ response to 1NT opening. If the opener rebids with the responder's four carder major on 2 ♣ response, then the responder should decide whether to jump to a game or a slam, depending upon his/her count strength and length of suits. 2 ♣ response to a 1NT opening leaves many options open to the responder and the player can plan appropriate strategy at a later stage.

3.4.6 Responder with strong hands :

The responder is fortunate to look at strong hands, with 16 HCP or more, with or without a long suit, whenever his/her partner has opened with 1 NT.

a) Strong hands with long suits are easier to bid since the responder has a 2 ♣ option to know the cards distribution, and the count range of the opener opening 1NT. After estimating the same responder may choose to ask Aces and reach a game or a slam.

b) The responder can also give a jump bid into the long suit first and then plan to bid a slam in the longer suit.

c) If the responder has 16 or more HCP and wants to estimate a slam, then similar route of first forcing with 2 ♣ and then planning a slam is better.

d) Avoid blind bids of responding with 4NT or 5NT, whatever may be your count strength. Choose a 2 ♣ route. The partnership understanding may allow them to do a lot of variations in this bidding system.

❖ ❖ ❖

Engineering System
Exercise No. 3: Bidding Beyond First Round

Note :

1. Please go through the earlier chapters carefully and then answer the following questions.

2. For each of the question, answer precisely.

3. You are dealt with a hand which is described in each question.

   Your opening bid and a response by your partner is also given. Your job is to explain, on the basis of partners' response, the HCP and probable distribution of cards with the partner and propose your bid.

4. Assume bidding is not interrupted by opponents.

Example No. 1 - You hold the following hand

♠ - AK83, ♥ - K52, ♦ - J, ♣ - KQJ93

and you have opened one Club. Give your opinion on the following points, if your partner responds with either of the following:

a) 1 ♦, or b) 1 ♥, or c) 2 ♣, or d) 1 NT, or e) 2 ♦

Q - 1.   Are you in a part game or a game zone?

2.   What will you bid now, for each of the responses, as stated above?

3.   Are you sure that, with your last bid, the partner will be in a position to estimate correctly, whether you have a contract in a game / part-game zone ?

4.   What responses do you anticipate from your partner, to your bid, as stated in (2) above.

Ex. 2 - For each of the first response stated in Example 1 above, if your partner holds the following cards correspondingly then, what should be the final contract ? What could be the sequence of bidding?

a) ♠ – T96, ♥ – AQJ63, ♦ – 94, ♣ – T74,

b) ♠ – JT6, ♥ – AQJ63, ♦ – Q9, ♣ – T74

c) ♠ – JT62, ♥ – AQJ6, ♦ – Q4, ♣ – T74

d) ♠ – JT62, ♥ – AQJ, ♦ – QT98, ♣ – T7

e) ♠ - J, ♥ – AQJ6, ♦ – KT9872, ♣ – T7

❖ ❖ ❖

Engineering System
Bidding Beyond First Round – Answers to
Exercise No. 3

Comments on solutions to Exercise No. 3

You hold the hand given in Example No. I and your partner holds the cards described in Example No. 2.

You have opened I ♣. You have 17 HCP, 3½ tricks, a five carder ♣ suit, a four carder ♠ suit and a singleton ♦ Jack. This count is a waste unless partner has that suit with the other honors.

Let us look at each hand of the responder in Example No. 2.

a) Responder has seven HCP, I ½ trick, a five card ♥ suit and above all the count strength is concentrated in the longer suit. Even then, respond to a I ♣ opening with a I ♦. I ♣ opener may only pass your I ♦ response if the opener has a five card ♦ suit and only 13 - 15 HCP (3.2.1-C), in which case you would be in a part game zone and nothing to lose.

Opener	Responder
I ♣	I ♦
2 ♣ (p)	2 ♥ (q)
2 ♠ or 3 ♥ (r)	4 ♥ (s)

p - 2 ♣ is 13 to 18 HCP, 5 carder ♣ suit. Non forcing bid.

q - 2 ♥ is 5 card ♥ suit, 4 - 7 HCP, ready to play.

r - 2 ♠ - 4 card ♠, not joining in ♥, 15 - 18 HCP, and a five carder ♣, but 3 ♥ would indicate 15 - 18 HCP, joining 3 cards of ♥. Interested in game if the responder has a good suit, compatible hand.

s - If the opener rebids 3 ♥, bid a game. 6 - 7 HCP, good ♥ suit. A 3 carder ♣ Compatible hand. Game possible if the opener has 16 - 18 HCP. However if the opener responds with 2 ♠, then just 'pass'.

In this hand the first round bidding indicates only a part game but subsequent bids help them to learn more about HCP and cards distribution reaching a game.

(b) **Opener**   **Responder**
    1 ♣   1 ♥ (p)
    2 ♣ (q)   2 ♥ (r) or 3 ♥ (s)
    2 ♠ (t), 3 ♥ (u) or 2NT(v)

p - 8 – 11 HCP, some 5 card suit.

q - 5 card ♣ suit, unlimited, interested in knowing partner's 5 card suit.

If the opener bids a five card major suit, it is expected that the responder should indicate a 3 card join in the opener's suit, rather than bidding his/her five card suit.

r - 2 ♥ – 5 ♥ card suit. Non forcing. Ready to stop.

s - 3 ♥ – 6 ♥ card or longer good suit, 10 - 11 HCP Interested in a game if the opener joins.

t - To a 2 ♥ response if the opener rebids 2 ♠, it would indicate 5 card ♣, 4 card ♠ and 16 or more HCP, but no ♥ join.

u - To 2 ♥ response, a 3 ♥ response would indicate a 3 card support and a minimum hand i.e. 13 - 14 HCP, Non forcing. It is up to the responder to bid a game depending on the responder's count strength and cards distribution.

v - On 2 ♥ response, if the opener bids 2NT, it is also controlling ♠ and ♦. Interested in 3NT if the responder has 10 HCP and quality of hand is satisfactory.

On a 3 ♥ response by the responder, the opener may bid a game in 3NT or 4 ♥ or may ask Aces by 4 ♣. The responder should believe in the opener and respond accordingly.

So bidding for the hand in the exercise would be:

Opener	Responder
1 ♣	1♥ (8 – 11 HCP. Some five card suit)
2 ♣	2 ♥ Heart suit
4 ♣ (Ace asking, Over ambitious)	4 ♥ (showing one Ace)
Pass (Happy to stop)	

A one ♥ response cannot include all three Aces (12 HCP). 10 - 11 HCP may include two Aces but may or may not include good ♥ suit quality. If anything of ♥ - A,

Q or J are missing, then conducting four ♥ would be tough. So asking Aces by opener is over ambitious. One should simply bid 4 ♥ indicating ♥ support, 15+ HCP (because 2 ♥ response may also have 8 - 9 HCP).

(c) In this particular hand, the opener receives a 2 ♣ response indicating 8 - 11 HCP and minimum four cards in each major, then opener should give a game forcing bid. Opener has 17 HCP and even with 8 HCP with the 2 ♣ responder, a game in 4 ♠ has to be bid. Since the opener has a four card AK in ♠ but 3 card K in ♥ and singleton ♦.

It is tempting to know whether the responder has a hand like:

♠ – QJXX ♥ – AQJXX ♦ – XX ♣ – T8 or

♠ – T9XX ♥ – AQJXX ♦ – AX etc.

The opener sees a loser in Spade, Diamond and Clubs or Hearts if there is one Ace with the responder. Slam is a remote possibility (just like in case 'b' above). It would be over ambitious to give Ace asking bid of 4 ♣, however a 2 ♠ bid to 2 ♣ response would only indicate a four card Spade suit and 13 - 14 HCP.

Even with 2 ♠ bid, a responder may bid 3 ♥ indicating 5 carder ♥ and four carder ♠ or may respond 3 ♠. Both bids would indicate 10 - 11 HCP asking opener to bid a game if the quality of the opener's hand is satisfactory.

On 2 ♠ bid of the opener, a 3 ♣ or 3 ♦ bid by responder would indicate 10 - 11 HCP and a four card minor bid suit in addition to both four carder majors.

The recommended bidding is as follows:

Opener	Responder
1 ♣	2 ♣
3 ♠ – game force	4 ♠ – Game bid. Stop bid. Nothing more.

A 4 ♥ bid here would indicate 5 card solid suit of ♥, 10 - 11 HCP and good 4 cards in ♠. HCP concentrated necessarily in ♥ and ♠ suits.

(d) The responder's hand qualifies for 1NT response. In this hand if a ♦ suit is changed to four small cards, i.e. the HCP for ♦ Q are missing (and even T9 is missing) then although the hand has 8 HCP, it is recommended that the responder should give 1 ♦ bid and subsequently indicate the maxima by bidding a four carder suit in competitive bidding.

On 1NT response, the opener is supposed to bid 2 ♣ which is to be interpreted as asking a four carder suit. In case of a 2 ♦ response, it will indicate a four card ♦ suit but will also indicate that there is no four card major suit. Please refer to 3.2.3.

The recommended bidding is:

Opener	Responder
1 ♣	1NT – 9 – 11 HCP, balanced hand.
2 ♣	2 ♠ – four carder Spade
4 ♠ Shut bid. Maximum Hand. Happy to bid a game with four card ♠ suit.	

The opener has 17 HCP and 5 card ♣ suit but is worried about ♦ – suit and has a four card major suit. Bidding 3 ♣ to indicate maximum hand would be risky. Since 2 ♣ is a forcing bid opener can correct the course of bidding (to indicate 17 HCP) at later stage explained below:

Opener	Responder
1 ♣	1 NT
2 ♣	2 ♦ (if suppose it is a response, no major four carder).

then

      2 ♠ here would indicate four card ♠ and also 15 - 16 HCP.

Or   3 ♣ bid here would indicate 4 or 5 card ♣ suit. A sign off. Stop bid.
Interested in Playing 3 ♣

Or   2NT bid here would show one major control 15 - 16 HCP interest in playing 3NT if responder has 10 - 11 HCP.

NOTE: The bidding may also take a shape like:-

Opener	Responder
1 ♣	1N
2 ♣	2 ♥ (assume, if)

2NT or 3 ♣ here would again indicate as described above.

(e) It is a typical hand. The responder may have against 1 ♣ opening.

The responder has to bid a longer or higher of two five carder suits. The response here would be 2 ♦.

If the opener has 13 - 14 HCP, then even with 11 HCP a game is not seen unless the responder has a five carder major where the opener may have a solid 3 or 4 card join. The opener may bid a suit to give a relay or may pass with doubleton join to keep the bidding low. A 2 NT bid would encourage the responder to bid his/her second suit for which the opener must have 15 - 17 HCP. Even a change in level would be an invitation for a game. A 3 ♦ rebid by the opener would be a border line for 3NT game if the responder has 10 - 11 HCP.

The recommended bidding is as follows:

Opener	Responder
1 ♣	2 ♦ Longer or higher of two five carder suits.
2NT forcing	3 ♥ Second suit
(ref. 3.2.5)	(obviously four carder)
3NT Stop bid	

Special Notes :-

1. A hand with 15 – 17 HCP and 5 – 4 - 3 – 1 distribution offers a lot of flexibility in bidding.

2. A responder having 12 HCP and whatever distribution, must initially give a game forcing 1 ♠ response, and then explore the possibility of correct suit contract, No-trump contract or slam contracts.

3. A rebid of any suit by the opener or a responder indicates a six card suit. (Except in 'two suiter' openings where immediate rebid indicates 7 - 3 distribution).

4. On a 1 ♠ response to 1 ♣ or 1 ♦ opening, the opener and responder should indicate 5 carder suits and then a four carder so as to reach the proper contracts.

5. Hands full of T98s are more valuable although a count value is not assigned to these cards. These cards improve quality of hand.

6. Solid suit means sequential suit without gaps and a good five card suit means a five card suit headed by two top honors A, K or Q.

7. For 'two suiter' hands length and hierarchy is important Major suit game contracts require 10 tricks as against 11 tricks in minor suit game contract.

8. For a suit contract, the partners together should have eight cards of trump suit to make a game along with count-strength as explained earlier.

9. The opener should listen to the response of the partner, and then bid either his /her own five card suit or No trump, if the opener has no suit.

10. If the responder shows a suit, the opener can join his/her suit with three cards, but must give a game forcing bid if the opener knows that both hands together have enough HCP for a game bid.

11. Bid a game as soon as you realize that you and your partner have a minimum of eight cards in agreed suit with enough HCP to make a game.

12. If you think, you jointly have about 30 HCP or more, it is better to find out if you together have all Aces and Kings, before you bid a slam.

13. Whenever you want to know how many Aces your partner is having, give a 4C bid, which is an Ace asking bid as per the "Gerber" convention. Remember you must possess at least one Ace.

14. If your partner bids 4 ♣ to ask you your Aces, then reply as follows :-

    1. 4 ♦   -   No Ace

    2. 4 ♥   -   One Ace

    3. 4 ♠   -   Two Aces

    4. 4Nt   -   Three Aces

15. Use DOPI convention if there is an intervention from RHO, if the partner has asked Aces (or Kings). It means if RHO gives any bid, then, if you double that suit, it would be indicating "no Ace", on the other hand, if you 'pass' it would indicate "one Ace". Similarly, a bid of next higher suit of RHO, at the same level, would indicate "two Aces" and so on.

16. Similarly 5 ♣ can be used as a King asking bid which must be answered on the same lines.

17. There are many other Ace asking/responding conventions available which may also be utilized with due partnership understanding.

□□□

Special Tip 2:

- With this knowledge start playing and practicing now!

- Read, while you play, for reference.

REAL LIFE ADVENTURES
by GARY WISE & LANCE ALDRICH

SOUTH LED WITH THE SPADE KING AND WEST SIGNALED WITH THE SEVEN, CONVINCING SOUTH HE HAD A DOUBLETON, AFTER THE ACE AND ANOTHER SPADE, SOUTH RUFFED IN DUMMY.

Bridge: the perfect game for those who don't find quantum physics challenging enough.

BRIDGE PLAYERS

KNOW HOW TO FINESSE
THE WAY TO THE TOP

Opening Unbalanced Hands
'Two suiter' Openings & Responses

4.1   Introduction

Anybody can easily understand that Bridge is a funny management game. Funny because it can defy any principles laid down for the game. You may get cards dealt to you, which could fetch you many more or much less tricks than you anticipate during the bidding.

It becomes very important to handle cards dealt to you, which are unbalanced hands. On many occasions you get hands with a singleton or doubleton in a suit. If your partner has a long suit, which is your singleton then you may land in a difficulty.

It is also likely that you have a long suit in which your partner also has triple-ton or more cards. You may reach a game bid and fulfill it just because of distribution of cards without having enough count-strength.

To take care of unbalanced hands, "Engineering System" has introduced 'two suiter' responses (introduced in Chapter No. 2.2.e or 2.3.e) as well as 'two suiter' openings, which are being described now.

4.2   Weak 'Two suiter' Opening Calls:

4.2.1   A 'Two Suiter' hand is defined as the cards dealt to you, which have a minimum of ten cards in two suits only. You may have more too. i.e. the distribution of cards in various suits could be

a) 5 – 5 - 2 – 1, 5 – 5 – 3 – 0   Or

b) 6 – 4 – 2 – 1, 6 – 4 – 3 – 0, 6 – 5 – 2 – 0   Or

c) 7 – 3 – 3 – 0, 7 – 3 – 2 – 1 Or 7 – 4 – 2 – 0 etc.

Please note that in an unbalanced hand, a distribution of cards like 7 – 2 – 2 – 2 Or 8 – 2 – 2 – 1, etc. should not be considered as a 'two suiter' hand. The unbalanced hand may have a distribution like 13 – 0 – 0 – 0 at its extreme.

All the unbalanced hands, where there are a minimum of ten cards in two suits and each of the suits have three or more cards, can be treated as 'two suiter' hands. Please note that if you have a distribution like 8 – 2 – 2 – 1, then you must open with 1 ♣, if the hand satisfies the conditions, or you must give a pre-emptive bid to show your hand, which will be described later.

4.2.2   Look at the following hands which are the typical examples of 'two suiter' hands :

a) ♠ – 5, ♥ – K 7 3, ♦ – A Q T 9 8 3 2, ♣ – A 6

Seven carder ♦, Three Carder ♥.

b) ♠ – K -3, ♥ – Q J T 9 6 2, ♦ – K, ♣ – Q J 5 4

Six carder ♥, Four carder ♣.

c) ♠ – A K T 8 7, ♥ – Q J T 9 8 7, ♦ - Nil , ♣ – Q J

Five carder ♠ and Six carder ♥.

d) ♠ - Nil, ♥ – 5, 2, ♦ – K Q T 9 8, ♣ – A K T 9 8 3

Five carder ♦ and Six carder ♣.

4.2.3 Opening calls for a weak 'two suiter' hands :-

a) Opening a weak 'two suiter' requires 11 – 15 HCP and at least ten cards in two suits.

b) If suits are distributed 5 – 5 or 6 – 4, then call a higher suit of the two suits first, e.g. if you have ♠ 4 cards and ♥ 6 cards, bid 1 ♠ if HCP are 11 – 15 only.

c) Opening bids for 'two suiter' calls are restricted to be 1 ♥, 1 ♠, 2 ♣ and 2 ♦. Any of these bids by the opener assures minimum four cards in a bid suit and also assures existence of another suit as well as minimum Eleven HCP.

d) If the opener bids higher suit first and lower suit later then it indicates a count range of 11 - 15 only.

For example:

	Opener	Responder
1)	1 ♥	1 ♠
	2 ♣ i.e. First ♥ & then ♣	
	OR	
2)	1 ♠	1 Nt
	2 ♥ i.e. First ♠ & then ♥.	
	OR	
3)	2 ♦	2 ♥
	3 ♣ i.e. First ♦ & then ♣.	

All these bids show two suits with a count range of 11 - 15 only. (Responses as described in 4.5)

4.3   Strong 'two suiter's -

If 'two suiter' hands have a count value of more than 15 HCP i.e. 16 HCP and above, then the opener should open a lower suit first and then bid the higher suit.

For example:

	Opener	Responder
a)	1 ♥	1 ♠*
	2 ♠ (♠ is Higher suit than ♥s)	
b)	2 ♦	2 ♥
	2 ♠	

1 ♥ opening assures a minimum four carder Heart and 2 ♠ bid shows second suit as ♠ with minimum four cards which means the opener has a minimum of ten cards in ♥s and ♠s together.

(* NOTE : Please refer 4.7 e.g.9)

It is therefore clearly understood that if the opener gives 1 ♠ bid, then it is a 'two suiter' bid, and since ♠ is the highest suit in hierarchy, the next suit shall only be a lower one and therefore the count strength is between 11 to 15 only. Hence 1 ♠ is always a weak two suit opening.

On similar lines, it could be easily understood that Clubs being the lower-most suit, in the hierarchy, a 2 ♣ opening will always indicate strong 'two suiter' hand guarantying 16 plus HCP and a minimum of four carder Club suit.

4.5   Responding to 'two suiter' openings –

a) Remember the descending hierarchy of suits i.e. ♠, ♥, ♦ & ♣.

b) It is very important to communicate a better fit of suits as well as count strength to each other. For bidding a Game or a Slam, the control could be taken over by the opener or the responder, depending upon who has a correct knowledge of the HCP strength and length of suits in both of the hands.

c) Generally, a first response to a 'two suiter' opening is a relay (a next immediate un-bid suit or no-trump, bid at the same level) asking the opener to bid the next suit. This gives you clarity of suits as well as strength of HCP. On the basis of this, responder can give one more relay (as stated above) to know the length of each suit, i.e. minimum 5 - 5 or 6 - 4, etc.

d) The opener may rebid a longer suit in the third round, if distribution is 6 - 4, or give a relay (as stated above) to indicate minimum 5 - 5 cards in each suit.

e) This is a stage where responder has to decide whether to go for a Game or a Slam, based on the responder's strength, and should ask Aces/Kings by any convention.

   If one of the bid suits is a Club suit then partners may decide to use the Blackwood convention for Ace asking in such specific cases to avoid any confusion.

f) If the opener is a weak 'two suiter' and the responder is also weak - less than eight HCP - then the responder should decide whether to stop immediately with a proper fit or at the minimum misfit.

g) Relay bid is nothing but a next immediate suit bid. This allows the partners to continue bidding without losing much of a bidding space.

| 4.6 | Let us illustrate this with simple examples. |

Illustration - I

	Opener	Responder
The Hands	♠ – A K T 8 7	♠ – Q 6 4 3
	♥ – Q J T 9 8 7	♥ – A 6 4
	♦ - Nil	♦ – A J 7
	♣ – Q J	♣ – 6 5 2
The bidding -	1 ♠	1 NT(a)
	2 ♥	2 NT(b)
	3 ♣ (c)	

a) 1 NT
- a Relay bid
- Responder knows there is a good fit in ♠ because opener must be having a minimum four carder ♠.
- Responder also knows that the opener has 11 - 15 HCP.
- Responder in general has following options: Bid 2 ♠ with 0 - 8 HCP with at least four carder ♠ or give a relay bid of 1 NT to know more about opener, if the responder has 9 or more HCP.

b) 2 NT
- Opener has shown two suits, ♠ and ♥. This bid asks the opener to describe length of each suit. If the opener rebids any of these suits, then the rebid suit has six cards and the other bid suit has four cards.

c) 3 ♣
- It is a relay bid to indicate that the opener is having a minimum of 5 - 5 cards in each of the bid suits.

You have to now decide whether to bid a game or a Slam, and whether that should be in Hearts or Spades, as you are joining in both of the suits. Please note that opener will not open his/her mouth anymore as he/she has given all the information. The opener shall respond only to Ace asking call of 4 ♣.

	Opener	Responder	
e.g. 1)	1 ♥	1 ♠	Unlimited Relay bid. Responder is just waiting. Need not have a single card of ♠.
e.g. 2)	1 ♥	1 NT	Indicates 8+ HCP.
e.g. 3)	1 ♥	2 ♣	It is a positive response. Must have five carder ♣ suit and 12+ HCP.
e.g. 4)	1 ♥	2 ♥	Four card ♥ support. 6 – 8 HCP. Weak. Non forcing. Ready to stop.

Additional Notes :-

- For a one Heart opening, if the responder has a five carder Diamond suit, regardless of count strength, it is preferred to or rather advised to give a waiting call of 1 ♠, because in case the opener has ♥ and ♣ suits, your response of 2 ♦ over 1♥ opening will force the opener to bid Clubs at 3 ♣ level. This will reduce a bidding space. If you have a strong hand, a four carder ♥ and a five carder ♦, then you may venture to bid 2 ♦.

- Avoid bidding 3 ♥ or 4 ♥ even if you have four / five carder ♥ suit and good count strength. Give a relay bid, which is forcing the opener to bid next suit allowing you to know whether opener has a strong or weak hand. But the moment opener has disclosed both the suits, it is the responder who has a better estimate of total HCP strength of both hands together and hence the responder should take over the control of bidding, force the bidding to reach at necessary level of contract, and use Ace askinging bid if necessary.

	Opener	Responder	
e.g. 5)	1 ♥	1 ♠ *	* Waiting. A relay bid.
	2 ♦	Pass	0 to 4 HCP, at least three carder ♦ support. No ♥ support.
e.g. 6)	1 ♥	1 ♠ *	* Waiting. A relay bid.
	2 ♦	2 ♥	5 - 8 HCP, at least a triple-ton / doubleton ♥. No ♦ support (singleton /void). A sign off.

	Opener	Responder	
e.g. 7)	1 ♥	1 ♠ *	* Relay bid
	2 ♦	2 ♠	A game force. Indicate a five carder ♠. Asking the opener to describehis/her distribution
	2 NT		Next immediate bid on asking bid means the opener guarantees a minimum of five cards in each of the bid suits.
e.g. 8)	2 ♦	2 ♥ *	* Waiting, nothing to do with ♥ Suit.

	3 ♣	!	One can use same responses as in Example 7 above like Pass or 3 ♦ for weak hands. (0 - 10) HCP.
			Bid 3 ♥ to indicate 5 card ♥ with 12 + count
			Bid 3 ♠ to indicate 5 card Spade suit with 12+ HCP.
			Bid 4 NT (Blackwood) to ask Aces.
e.g. 9)	2 ♦	2 ♥	Relay Bid
	2NT	----	The opener shows that his/her other suit is ♥s and has minimum five cards in ♦s and ♥s. Strong hand 16+ HCP is a forcing bid. A three ♥ bid would have shown 6 – 4 distribution in favour of ♥ and a strong 'two suiter'.
e.g.10)	2 ♦	2 ♥	Relay bid
	2 ♠		The opener is indicating a strong hand with Spades as the other suit. The responder may ask :

			a) Distribution by next immediate bid (2 NT) here to know the length of suits. If the opener rebids any of his/her bid suit, then the bid suit is a six carder suit and the other suit has four cards. However on 2 NT asking, if the opener bids any other suit, not previously bid by him/her, then there are minimum five cards, in each of the suits bid by the opener.
			b) plan to bid a game
			c) May bid a slam as explained in e.g. 9. The control of bidding must be taken over by the responder. The responder should choose forcing/non-forcing or sign off bids.

4.8   Hands with Longer suit:

At times a 'two suiter' hand may have peculiar cards distribution like 7 - 3 - 3 - 0 OR 7 - 3 - 2 - 1

In such cases you have to decide whether your hand fits into i) a strong 'two suiter' (16 + HCP) or ii) a weak 'two suiter' or iii) a hand suitable for a pre-emptive bid.

(i) In a case of a weak 'two suiter' hand, open a seven carder suit (1 ♥, 1 ♠, 2 ♣, 2 ♦ – depending on the suit) and repeat the same suit to indicate seven carder hand with 11-15 HCP.

(ii) It is better to open a strong 'two suiter' hand with one Club opening as you can estimate partner's HCP as well as distribution easily which would allow you to reach a game or slam in appropriate suits.

(iii) A pre-emptive bid is described as follows:

In case you have a less than 12 HCP and an unbalanced hand with a 7 carder suit, then you are eligible to give a pre-emptive bid in the longer suit.

If your partner has passed, or you think you are in a favorable vulnerability and want to create a barrier in the bidding space for the opponents, then use a pre-emptive bid. If you have at least seven cards in a suit, around nine HCP (8 -11) and have one probable entry in the side suits (un-bid suits) the pre-emptive bid should be made with bids like 2 ♥, 2 ♠, 3 ♣, 3 ♦. Remember 1 ♥ or 1 ♠ or 2 ♦ or 2 ♣ is a natural 'two suiter' bid, as per this convention.

Note that a pre-emptive bid is an opening call only. Avoid bidding it at first or forth position, unless you are in a favorable vulnerability, when all others have passed. First or third position is appropriate, with a favorable vulnerability when partner and RHO have not bid. It may allow the partner to grab an opportunity of bidding a game at minimum HCP.

Look at the illustration below:

Let us say that you are West and have the following hand, when the opponents are vulnerable.

♠	–	KQ
♥	-	K J 8 6 5 4 3
♦	-	5 4 3
♣	-	J

Assume your partner, as a dealer, has passed and the RHO (South) also passes. It is your turn to bid. It is quite likely that North (LHO) may have one Club opening and the deal may be in favor of N – S. It could also be a vulnerable game for them.

This is the right opportunity. Bid pre-emptive. Bid 2 ♥. 1 ♥ is a 'two suiter' opening but 2 ♥ is a pre-emptive one. If your partner has 11-12 HCP and marginal ♥ support with a strong side suit, he/she can bid a game easily or may decide to sacrifice, against the opponents bidding, with a weaker hand.

Please note once you open a pre-emptive bid you should not bid again in subsequent rounds unless your partner forces you with an Ace asking bid.

Note that 2 ♥, 2 ♠, 3 ♣, 3 ♦ are pre-emptive bids. Since these are jump bids you must alert the opponents by taping the table by fingers and saying 'Stop' before you bid the pre-emptive like 'Stop – Two Hearts' in the case above.

Following are typical hands suitable for pre-emptive bids.

1) ♠ - A K x x x x x
   ♥ - x x x
   ♦ - xx
   ♣ - x
   Bid – 2 ♠

2) ♠ – x x x
   ♥ – A x
   ♦ - K J T 9 8 x x
   ♣ – x
   Bid – 3 ♦

❑❑❑

BRIDGE

IS AN
INTELLECTUAL GAME

Competitive Bidding
After Interventions

Of late the game of Bridge has become more and more competitive. You may find yourself playing it at home, in a pair's progressive tournament or in a Duplicate team event. Winning points for your side is always very important everywhere. You may earn the points either by proper bidding, playing and conducting the deal for fulfillment of the contract or push the opponents to bid a little too high and then defend properly to collect penalty by defeating them.

Often you look at hands which make you think that you should bid but your opponents have already entered the bidding and you start worrying how to communicate your hand with your partner for which you have need to change your strategy of opening calls. This is called Competitive Bidding.

5.2 Opening calls after interventions

Let us say you are dealt with a hand like:

♠ – AJX, ♥ – XX,

♦ – QJXXX, ♣ – KQX   (X indicates any small card)

You have thirteen HCP, two tricks, six pictures and a five carder ♦ suit and find yourself in the following bidding position.

	LHO	Partner	RHO	You	
a)	P	P	1 ♠	?	or
b)	1 ♣	P	1 ♥	?	

Should you bid after these interventions or not? Following are the illustrations to answer this question.

5.2.1 Simple Overcalls

In situation (a) above, the RHO is showing an opening hand with Spade suit in most of the bidding systems and a 'two suiter' hand as per our bidding convention. It is recommended here that you should bid two Diamonds. Since your bid is after an intervention your partner should take this bid as at least a five carder Diamond suit with 9 to 13 HCP and need not be a 'two suiter' hand. This bid is known as a "simple over call".

If your partner has (i) twelve HCP, then he/she should enter the bidding even after or without any intervention by your LHO on your 2 ♦ bid, as in the example stated above, by showing a five card suit; or (ii) simply raise your suit by one level if he/she has three carder support with only 8 - 11 HCP; or (iii) If weak, should keep quiet. Partner should also keep quiet if he/she has 8 -12 HCP but cannot fulfill above mentioned requirements (i.e. no three carder join in your suit and no biddable five carder suit) to collect penalty from the opponents.

(i) Like let's say your Partner holds a five carder Heart or Clubs suit with 11-12 HCP then he/she should bid the five carder suit if bidding sequence like 5.2.a has occurred and you have over called two Diamonds.

(ii) If your partner does or does not have some five carder suit but has a minimum three carder Diamond with 8–12 HCP, then the partner should raise your Diamond bid by one level e.g.

(c) | LHO | Partner | RHO | You |
|---|---|---|---|
| P | P | 1 ♠ | 2 ♦ |
| Any bid below 3 ♦ | Bid 3 ♦ | | |
| or pass | | | |

Make sure you don't cross level three (unless, of-course, if you want to sacrifice) as your partnership may not hold enough count strength to go to four level. Especially if you are vulnerable and opponents are not, then you and your partner should take due care while bidding.

5.2.2 In a situation 5.2.b) above, where opponents have shown a part game and you have thirteen HCP with a five carder Diamond and you bid 2 ♦ with of course a favourable vulnerability, then it is obvious that your opponents together have minimum 21 HCP and would be trying to estimate a cheap game (in majors or

No-trump with a Diamond control). In this situation, your partner has to be careful while bidding. Your partner may have 0 to 6 HCP and may sacrifice with lower HCP if vulnerability is favourable or wait for a penalty with higher HCP.

5.3 Examples: Let us say that bidding goes as follows

LHO	Partner	RHO	You
-	-	1 ♣	P
1 ♦ or / 1 ♥ or / 1 ♠	P	1 NT	?
(e) (f) (g)			

5.3.1   Take the situation (e) where LHO responds 1 ♦ to an opening call by RHO and your partner passes. This means that LHO has 0 to 8 HCP but RHO has 13 to 16 HCP.

Now,

(i)   if you have 9 to 13 HCP and a five carder suit then bid your suit at level two.

(ii) If you have 11 - 13 HCP and no five carder suit, 'Double' the NT bid by RHO forcing partner to bid at least a four carder suit at level two which will be a non-forcing bid for you.

5.3.2   In situation (f) the LHO has responded 1 ♥ to opening call of 1 ♣ by RHO indicating 8 - 11 HCP (Part game zone with some five carder suit), 1 NT. Re-bid could be a waiting (dangerous) bid by RHO and you may bid only if you have following.

(i) Bid a solid six card suit, headed by Ace or King and at least three of top five honors in the suit and

(ii) 10 to 12 HCP with a six carder suit and a side entry (i.e. Ace or protected King in other suit).

e.g. ♠ – AXX, ♥ – XX, ♦ – KQJXXX, ♣ – XX, then bid 2 ♦.

5.3.3 In situation (g) where LHO has bid 1♠ indicating 12 HCP or above and the RHO is not having any five carder suit, then it would normally take the opponents to a 3 NT game. Taking this into consideration, you should simply keep quiet and wait for the penalty. Give a bid at level 2 only for lead indication to your partner so that the partner can lead a top card in your bid suit, at the end of the auction, if he/she is on the lead.

5.4 Bidding strong hands after interventions :

If your RHO has opened the bidding or it is your turn to bid when opponents have opened the auction and you have 14 HCP or more then it is important to communicate it to your partner accurately. Watch the following situations:

	LHO	Partner	RHO	You
Case a)	-	-	1 ♣ or 1 ♦ or 1 NT	?
Case b)	1 ♣	P	1 ♦	?
Case c)	1 ♦	P	1 ♥	?
Case d)	1NT	P	P	?

In situation (a) it is the RHO who has opened the bidding, as per their convention; but interpreted as per our convention, either by (i) 1 ♣ unlimited bid or (ii) 1 ♦ limited bid with 12 to 16 HCP and also with some five carder suit or (iii) 1NT – which is a limited balanced hand (Pl. note, different systems may have different opening calls which could be interpreted as mentioned here).

In general even if the opponent pair is not following the Engineering System of bidding, their system would also have a weak (limited) or strong (unlimited) and balanced / unbalanced hand opening calls.

Your job is to identify the situation and communicate with your partner, accordingly.

5.4.1 Case (a): (i) If you have a hand worth opening 1 ♣ as per our convention and have 15 + HCP, then, give a "double" to the RHO's call. The responses to this "double" are described in next section 5.4.2.

OR (ii) If you have a hand worth opening 1 ♦, as per our convention, then bid your five carder suit at the minimum possible level.

OR (iii) If you have a hand worth opening 1 NT, as per our convention, then you may 'pass' (called as 'trap pass') or give a take-out 'double' and subsequently bid 'pass' to show a 'light double'.

For example, if the RHO has opened 1 ♣ or unlimited bid and you have, let us say, the following type of hand:

♠ – AX, ♥ – KQXX, ♦ – AQXX, ♣ – XXX

Since RHO is strong, your ♥ – KQ is safe and should win tricks if RHO has Ace (more likely). Your ♦ - AQ will probably catch ♦ K of RHO and hence, your hand of 15 HCP becomes more valuable. If your partner has a solid major suit with five or more HCP it could put you in a very strong position.

For such hands, bid a 'double' to RHO's opening call. This is known to be a 'Take out Double', indicating a call forcing your partner to bid any of his/her longest suit, other than the bid suit by the opponents. Your 'take out double' also indicates that you have a void or a singleton/doubleton in the suit bid by the opponents.

Note: If the opponents are using a system of opening natural suits, you may use following strategy as well :

x) Bid 1NT if you have 15+ HCP and one control in the opponents' natural suit bid. Balanced hand.

y) Give a one level higher bid in RHO's bid suit (Cue bid) to indicate singleton/void in RHO's bid suit and with a strong (un)balanced hand, 15+ HCP, 4 – 4 – 4 – 1 or 5 – 4 – 4 – 0 distribution.

5.4.1 **Case (b)** : Use a 'Take out Double' with strong hands (15+ HCP), or bid your five carder suit with 12 - 15 HCP. You may also use a 'light double' if your hand is weak and you have no five carder suit.

Use the same strategy for other two cases, (c) and (d).

5.4.2   Responses to a 'Take out Double' :

Remember, if your partner has forced you to bid, you must bid even with zero HCP. For example 1 ♣, 1 ♦ and 2 ♣ openings in this system are forcing bids to which you must respond. Similarly you should respond to the 'take out double'.

You can still 'pass' this forcing bid in the following two exceptional situations.

(m) Your partner gives take out double and your RHO bids like

LHO	Partner	RHO	You
1 ♣	Double	1 ♠	!

Or Redouble

The moment RHO has bid anything other than pass, you are 'free' from bidding after your partners 'take out double' as your partner anyway gets a bidding turn because of RHO's bid. Say 'pass' if you have nothing to bid, i.e. very weak and/or no suit to bid.

(n) The other situation when you can pass a 'take out double' is

LHO	Partner	RHO	You
1 ♠	Double	P	?

You may pass if you are very weak (0 - 6 HCP) and have a solid and/or a long length of cards in the bid suit of LHO, after the partner bids a 'take out double', e.g. if you hold ♠ - QJT9XX. Especially when the opponents do not fetch a doubled game and you don't seem to make even a part game in any other suit, then you convert 'take out double' into a 'penalty double'.

However, except in cases 'm' and 'n' above you should respond to partners take out double as follows:-

e.g. (o)

	LHO	Partner	RHO	You
	1 ♣	Double	P	Case I
	1 ♦	Double	P	Case II
	1NT	Double	P	Case III

For all the cases above, respond as if your partner has opened the bidding by the call of LHO (which your partner has doubled), i.e. if partner doubles 1 ♣ of LHO, assume your partner has opened 1 ♣ and respond as per our conventions.

(p) In case LHO opens 1 ♥ or 1 ♠ which may be a natural suit bid and your partner doubles, bid your longer or better (other than LHO's) suit even if you are weak and free not to bid :

e.g.

	LHO	Partner	RHO	You
	1 ♥ or 1 ♠	Double	Redouble	Free Bid

Or bid 1 NT, if permissible, with 8 HCP and balanced hand with 4 cards in LHO's suit only or at least one control in LHO's suit.

e.g.

	LHO	Partner	RHO	You
	1 ♥ or 1 ♠	Double	P	Bid 1NT- with 8 HCP balanced hand one control in LHO's suit.

Or bid one step higher level, a jump bid, if you have 9 or 10 points.

e.g.	LHO	Partner	RHO	You
(I)	1 ♥	Double	P	2 NT 9 - 10 HCP ♥ control.
(II)	1 ♥	Double	P	2 ♠ 9 - 10 HCP 5 card ♠ suit.
(III)	1 ♠	Double	P	3 ♦ 9 - 10 HCP 5 card ♦ suit.

Or you may choose to force your partner to show his/her four card suit if you are short (singleton/void) in LHO's suit or you have a very strong hand, 11+ HCP.

For this you may bid the same suit as LHO at one level higher

i.e. LHO	Partner	RHO	You Bid
1 ♥	Double	P	2 ♥* * This is known as a 'cue bid'
or 2 ♦	Double	P	3 ♦* etc.

5.5

Look at the situations where you have intervention after the first response of your partner, e.g.

	You	LHO	Partner	RHO
Case-I	1 ♣	P	1 ♦	1 ♠

Case-II	1 ♦	P	1 N	2 ♦
Case-III	1 ♣	P	1 ♠	2 ♠
Case-IV	1 NT	P	2 ♦	2 ♥
Case-V	1 ♠	P	1 NT	2 ♥

We have to analyze each case separately before you bid after the intervention of RHO. To analyze, you must first look at the vulnerability of both parties and take a judgment if your total count strength after partner's first response is enough to fetch you a game, a part game or whether it is better to look for gaining penalty from the opponents.

5.5.1 In Case-I, your partner has indicated 0 to 8 HCP. It is a part game zone if you have less than 18 - 20 HCP. a) You should simply bid your five card suit at the minimum permissible level if you have 13 - 17 HCP, b) Bid it with jump raise if you have 18 or more HCP, c) Bid one No-trump if you have 16 or more HCP and one control in RHO's bid suit (i.e. A or Double ton K), d) Double the RHO's bid if you have 15 or more HCP but no control in RHO's suit and no five card suit, e) You can cue bid in RHO's suit if you have very strong game going hand but you want to know partners long suit, f) Bid 2 NT, if you have 20 or more HCP, two controls in RHO's bid suit.

The further action is left to the partner once you communicate your strength after RHO's intervention.

5.5.2 In case-II, you have opened weak, 12 - 16 HCP and some five carder suit and partner has already indicated 9 - 11 HCP with balanced hand, assuring a part game zone if you are minimum but probable game zone if both are maximum and join in a major

a) You should simply bid your suit at lowest level with 13 - 14 HCP.

b) You may give a jump bid if you have a strong six card major suit with 15 - 16 HCP.

5.5.3 In the case – III, your partner has indicated a game zone and you have a game in hand. RHO is crowding the bidding space by pushing you to level three. It is probably a preparation for their sacrifice bid having long 6 - 7 carder Spade with at least two top honours. In such a case act as follows:

a) Pass if you have no five card suit and 13 - 14 HCP, giving opportunity to your partner to bid his suit, if any. Partner may bid 2 NT with one control in Spade and no five carder suit. Partner should not pass, should at least bid a takeout double.

b) You can use a take out double with 15 HCP or more and singleton/doubleton Spade i.e. 4 – 4 – 3 – 2 distribution.

c) Bid 2 NT with two Spade controls and 15 HCP or more (even with ♠ – QJTX holding)

5.5.4 In case No. IV, your partner has signed off with 2 ♦, indicating a weak five card ♦ suit – 2 ♥ by RHO is a simple overcall indicating 10 or more HCP and a five card ♥ suit.

a) Bid 3 ♦ if you have at least 3 carder join in the suit.

b) Bid 2 ♠ with at least four carder ♠ and no three cards in ♦, 14 HCP or more.

c) Pass – no join in ♦, weak 12 - 13 HCP, no good quality

biddable major suit (not even QJTX of a major).

5.5.5   Case No. V is a 'two suiter' opening bid by you, 11 to 15 HCP, responded with a relay bid by your partner and then intervened by RHO with a simple overcall of 2 ♥ indicating 10 or more HCP and a five card Heart suit. Obviously your bidding gets congested and you have to bid your next suit at level three.

a) Pass with a five card Spade suit and 11 – 13 HCP. Allow your partner to either join Spades with three cards, remaining in part game zone or partner can bid his suit with 10 HCP (or more) or partner can bid 2N with at least one control in RHO's suit or partner can double opponent for penalty of which you may retain the double for penalty or take out by other suit depending upon your holding in RHO's suit and your count strength.

b) Rebid six carder Spade with 11 - 13 HCP.

c) Bid second suit (minimum five cards) and 14 - 15 HCP if it is different from RHO's suit.

    This bidding will allow partner also to have a lot of flexibility to choose calls from and settle at lower level in a part game zone.

d) Bid 2 NT with double control over RHO's suit and your second suit is RHO's suit with 14 - 15 HCP.

5.6

The following are some of the examples of bidding after intervention of a 'double' by RHO, when your partner has opened a call.

Partner	RHO	You	
1♣	Double	?	Case I
1♦	Double	?	Case II
1NT	Double	?	Case III
1♥ or 1♠ or 2♦	Double	?	Case IV
2♣	Double	?	Case V

Whenever your partner has opened 1♣ or 1♦ or 1NT and RHO doubles, then as per many bidding systems, your RHO is likely to have 14 HCP and more. Since your partner has about 13 HCP or more, then the other two hands, i.e. you and your LHO's will have to share remaining about 12 - 16 HCP.

In such a situation, it also means that, if you have Kings and Queens, then they will more often win the tricks. If you have AQ or KJ combinations, then you are likely to trap RHO's honors.

If you have 8 - 10 HCP, in such situations the value of hand will automatically improve and you may fetch a game even with little less HCP than what is prescribed in Chapter 2.

The responses will have to be modified to take advantage of two additionally available calls, i.e. 'Pass' and 'Re-double'. (Ref. 5.4.2.0)

Generally, 'Pass' is low 0 - 7 HCP. If on your 'pass', the LHO also passes and the opener does not have a five card suit or is worried in retaining the contract already doubled, then he/she should 're-double' to force you to bid your longer or better suit (even four cards). This is known as an 'S O S' re-double.

On RHO's double, if you re-double it would indicate a strong hand, ready to play in the opener's bid which is doubled by RHO. This will put the opponents in a tight corner and your LHO may be forced to bid a longer or better suit and if LHO passes, your RHO will be in a totally difficult position. In case you have a favorable vulnerability, such hands can give you good rewards.

5.6.1 Case I: Your partner has opened an unlimited bid 1 ♣. When RHO doubles you are free not to bid usual 1 ♦ response meaning 0 - 8 HCP to keep the bidding alive. You can simply 'pass', which would serve the purpose, instead of bidding anything.

a) If you bid 1 ♦ or 1 ♥ or 1 ♠ now, it would convey to your partner (Opener) that you have a five card bid suit (♦, ♥ or ♠) with 8 - 11 HCP. You can choose to 'pass' a five carder ♣ with 8 - 11 HCP.

b) The responses of 1NT or 2 ♣ or 2 ♦ or 2 ♥ or 2 ♠, would convey the same meaning as per our convention (as if RHO has not doubled), i.e. 1NT is a balanced hand with 9 - 11 HCP, 2 ♣ being both majors showing hand while remaining bids are 'two suiter' hands.

c) 'Re-double' should be used to show a game forcing strong response (12+ HCP).

5.6.2 Case II: 1 ♦ opener has a limited (12 - 16 HCP) hand with one five card suit. When RHO doubles, your partner, the opener, naturally gets an opportunity to bid his/her five card suit.

a) You should pass with 0 - 8 HCP as above.

b) Bid 1NT with 9 - 11 HCP and a balanced hand.

c) A bid of 1 ♥ or 1 ♠ would indicate 8 - 11 HCP with 5 carder bid suit with you.

d) Use re-double as a game forcing response (12+ HCP), asking your partner to bid his / her five carder suit (as you may have a balanced hand).

e) It is advisable not to use 'two suiter' responses in such situations, since you can ask your partner to bid his/her five carder suit by simply bidding a 'pass' and wait for the partner's suit bid.

5.6.3 **Case III:** Your partner has opened 1NT showing a balanced hand and 12 - 16 HCP.

a) If you have 0 - 8 HCP, a balanced hand, then just 'pass'.

b) If you have 8 - 11 HCP and a balanced hand, then bid 2 ♣ to ask a major or 'pass'.

c) If you have 5 - 11 HCP, a five card suit, then bid the same suit (sign off).

d) If you have 8 - 11 HCP and a six carder suit, give a 'jump bid' in that suit.

e) If you have 12+ HCP, then, redouble.

f) Stronger hands should be utilized to get the maximum benefit, either by bidding a redouble or try to encash the points from penalty from the opponents, by defeating their bid, or check if you have a game.

g) Take care of 'psyche' bids by the opponents, if you hold 16 HCP or more.

5.6.4 **Case-IV:** Your partner opens a 'two suiter' hand and your RHO doubles.

a) Simply use 'Pass' as a relay bid.

b) If you have a fitting hand, you may plan to join your partner at the earliest, as suggested below :

Your Partner	RHO	You
1 ♠	Double	4 ♠ (About 10 HCP)

This indicates a good four card ♠ join with two honors and a minimum hand. Try to steal the game preventing LHO to get any chance of communication. (Assume favourable vulnerability)

Your Partner	RHO	You
c) 1 ♥ or 1 ♠	Double	3 ♥ or 3 ♠.
		Game force. Strong four card join in the partner's bid suit with 9 - 12 HCP.

Your Partner	RHO	You
d) 2 ♦	Double	Redouble

This indicates 10 - 12 HCP, asking the partner to continue bidding. Partner should pass if ♦ is a six card suit with a minimum opening (12 - 14) HCP. Partner to bid the next suit if the other suit is a five carder. If the other suit is ♣ , then the partner has opened a 12 - 16 count hand. The partnership should decide the further course of action after practicing or experiencing such situations.

5.6.5 **Case- V:** Here it is obvious that the partner has 16 plus HCP and the ♣ suit may be a four card suit. Since the opponents are aware that your partner holds a strong 'two suiter' hand, the opponent (RHO) might offer a light or lead indicating double. If you are holding more than 9 HCP, then the game contract may be assured. Plan your bid on the basis of your length and or strength in ♣ suit. You may simply choose to pass with less than 9HCP, regardless of the distribution of cards in your hand. You may choose to bid 2NT with 9HCP and more, but not having 4 carder Clubs. You may bid 3 Clubs with 9HCP or more but having 4 carder Clubs. In both these cases the partner should either show a five/ six carder suit or choose to bid a game or slam, if Clubs are joining. If your card distribution is like 4 – 3 – 3 – 3 or 4 – 4 – 4 – 1 etc. then choose a suitable bid, e.g. you may choose to pass a weak hand with a minimum 3 carder Club, bid 2 NT with 9 or more HCP with a balanced distribution (at least doubleton Club) etc.

Practice will allow the partners to undergo such situations and then bidding may reach a stage where they may land at the 'Par' bids.

5.6.6 The bidding has to change based on the opponent's bidding system. To conclude, it should be noted that intervening calls could be either simple overcalls or smart bids to crowd your bidding. Generally, if you are vulnerable and opponents are not, then such a crowding will always be a possibility. Pre-emptive intervention is always a danger.

For example:

Partner	RHO	You	LHO
1 ♣	Pre-emptive		

a) In case you have 12 HCP or more, it is better to double indicating game zone to your partner.

b) If you have a five card suit, bid it with 8 - 11 HCP.

c) If you also have a pre-emptive biddable hand you may decide either to give a simple overcall or a jump over call.

d) It is better to pass with 0 - 8 HCP.

Based on partnership understanding you can develop your own bidding strategy to overcome the effect of interventions. This will also put you in a stronger position since you understand very well how to make intervening calls when opponents are vulnerable.

❑❑❑

Special Tip 3:

- After playing every deal, check your bidding with the partner.

- Find out if you have reached correct contract.

Annexure 1
Engineering System : Bidding Exercise No. 4

Q. 1: What is your opening bid if you have a following hand ? Write the answer in the block.

Answers -

☐ a) ♠ - A65432, ♥ – AQ, ♣ - Q54, ♦ - J4

☐ b) ♠ - AKQJ654, ♥ – 43, ♦ - K3, ♣ - 53

☐ c) ♠ - AKQJ, ♥ – 543, ♦ - J43, ♣ - Q54

☐ d) ♠ - A6543, ♥ – A53, ♦ - QJ3, ♣ - Q4

☐ e) ♠ - AKQJ5, ♥ – AQJ, ♦ - K, ♣ -KQJ2

Q.2: What will be your response if you have a following hand when your partner has opened with 'one Club'? Write your answer in the block.

☐ a) ♠ - T9, ♥ – KT987, ♦ - AT9, ♣ - Q54

☐ b) ♠ - T9, ♥ – KT, ♦ - AT987, ♣-AT98

☐ c) ♠ - T987, ♥ – T9876, ♦ - A, ♣- AT9

d) ♠ - T987, ♥ – KJT98, ♦ - A,   ♣ - AT9

e) ♠ - 87,   ♥ – KT98, ♦ - AT87, ♣ - AT9

Q. 3: You have a following hand and your partner has opened with 'one No-trump'. What will your response be? Write your answer in the block.

a) ♠ - T987, ♥ – KT987, ♦ - AT9,   ♣ - T

b) ♠ - T987, ♥ – K,   ♦ - AT9, ♣-A9876

c) ♠ - 87,   ♥ – KT987, ♦ - A,   ♣-A9876

d) ♠ - T9,   ♥ – KJT,   ♦ - AT9,   ♣ - A9876

e) ♠ - T9,   ♥ – K7,   ♦ - AT98, ♣-CT9876,

Answers to the Bidding Exercise No. 4

No.	Justification	Bid
Q.1		
a)	2 & ½ tricks, 13 HCP, 5 pictures	1 ♣
b)	2 & ½ tricks, 13 HCP, 5 pictures	1 ♣
c)	2 tricks, 13 HCP, 6 pictures	1 NT
d)	2 tricks, 13 HCP, 5 pictures, five carder suit	1 ♦
e)	5 tricks, 26 HCP, 11 pictures	1 ♣
Q.2		
a)	9 HCP, five carder suit ♥	1 ♥
b)	11 HCP, five carder suit ♦	1 ♥
c)	8 HCP, both majors, min. four cards each	2 ♣
d)	12 HCP, game force	1 ♠
e)	11 HCP, no five carder	1 NT

Q.3		
a)	7 HCP, five carder suit ♥	2 ♥
b)	11 HCP, five carder ♣, four carder ♠, forcing	2 ♣
c)	11 HCP, five carder ♥ & five carder ♣. It is a 'two suiter' hand. It is better to first give a forcing bid of two ♣s and if partner shows four carder ♥ then you are very happy but if he/she shows four carder ♠, you can bid 3 ♥s as you are having control cards in three suits, you are very well prepared for 3 NT If partner bids 2 ♦s or 2 NT, you can bid 3 ♥s.	2 ♣
d)	12 HCP, five carder ♣, you can give either a forcing bid of 2 ♣ or it is better to prefer to give 2 NT	2 NT
e)	7 HCP, five carder ♣	Pass

❑❑❑

Special Tip 4:

- Look at the deals in Annexure 2.

- Distribute the cards as indicated in the solved deals.

- Carry on your bidding and then check it with the book.

- Play the hand. It will give you more insight.

Annexure 2
Solved Deals

Bidding Example: 01

Deal No.: 14   Dealer: East   Vulnerable: None

Contract: Lead:

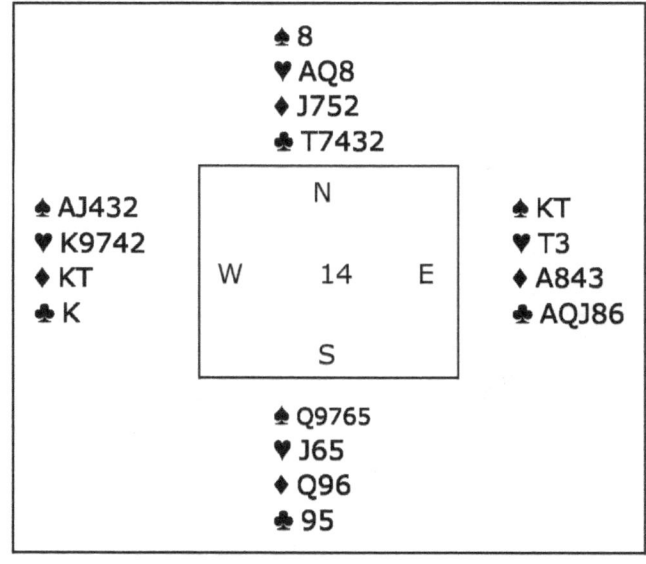

Bidding:

Dealer – East	South	West	North
1 ♣	P	1 ♠	P
2 ♣	P	2 ♠	P
3 ♣	P	3 ♥	P
3 NT	P	P	P

Suppose the dealer is switched :

Dealer – West	North	East	South
1 ♠	P	2 ♣	P
2 ♥	P	2 NT	P
3 ♦	P	3 NT	P
P	P	-	-

Explanation:

- If East is dealer, then East opens 1 ♣ and gets a game forcing response of 1 ♠.

- If West is dealer, West opens weak 2 suiter with 1 ♠. East responds with a game forcing 2 ♣.

- As a dealer, West shows both the suits in subsequent rounds and shows minimum five cards in each of the suits by bidding 3 ♦.

Bidding Example: 02

Deal No.: 07   Dealer: South   Vulnerable: Both

Contract: Lead:

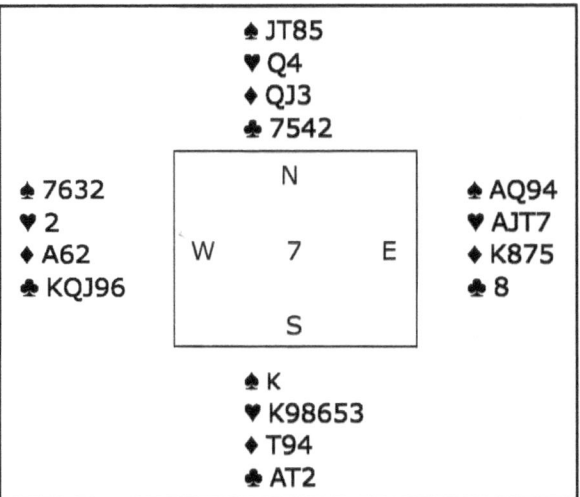

♠ JT85
♥ Q4
♦ QJ3
♣ 7542

♠ 7632
♥ 2
♦ A62
♣ KQJ96

N
W   7   E
S

♠ AQ94
♥ AJT7
♦ K875
♣ 8

♠ K
♥ K98653
♦ T94
♣ AT2

Bidding:

Dealer – South	West	North	East
P	P	P	1 ♣
P	1 ♥	P	1 NT
P	2 ♣	P	2 ♠
P	3 ♣	P	3 ♥
P	4 ♠	P	P
P	-	-	-

Explanation:

- East opens 1 ♣ and West responds for a part game zone with 1 ♥, as the HCP with West are less than 12 and has a five carder suit.

- East shows no five carder suit by 1 NT.

- West shows five carder ♣.

- East responds with four carder ♠ denying interest in ♣.

- West shows 3 ♣ again as the 2 ♣ bid may be interpreted as 'Stayman'.

- East continues to respond with four carder ♥.

- West has four carder ♠ and a good ♣ suit. So bids 4 ♠ game.

- Please note that if East opens, by mistake, with 1 NT, then also the bidding would be in similar sequence reaching a game in 4 ♠.

Bidding Example: 03

Deal No.: 10   Dealer: East   Vulnerable: Both

Contract: Lead:

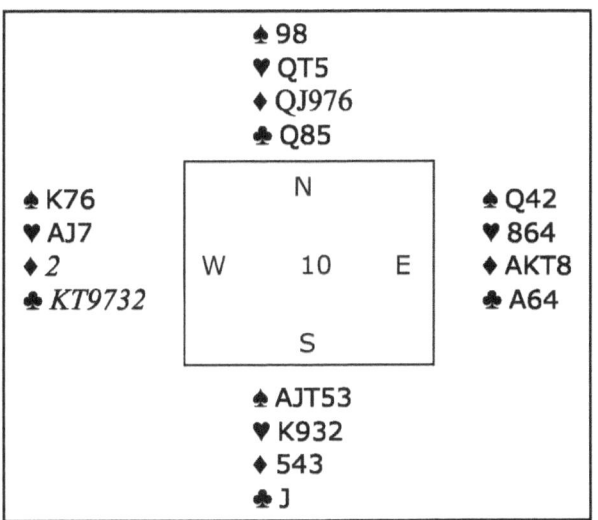

Bidding:

Dealer – East	South	West	North
I NT	P	2 ♣	P
2 ♦	P	3 ♣	P
3NT?	P	-	-

Explanation:

- East opens I NT and West gives a forcing response of 2 ♣.

- East denies major suit and indicates minimum with 2 ♦.

- West shows five carder ♣.

- East has a three carder Ace of ♣, 2 quick tricks in ♦ but just 13 HCP. So, in general, he/she should 'pass'.

- However, pairs may gamble with a 3 NT bid.

Special Tip 5:

- It is an interesting exercise to check what happens, in example 2 above, if South intervens by I ♥, after East opens with I ♣.

Bidding Example: 04

Deal No.: 07   Dealer: South   Vulnerable: Both

Contract: Lead:

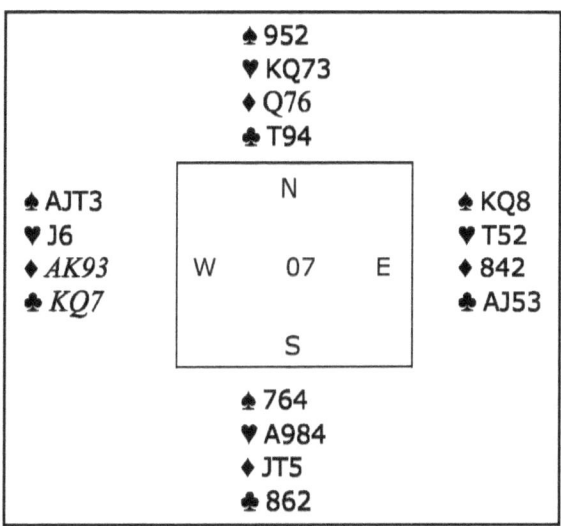

♠ 952
♥ KQ73
♦ Q76
♣ T94

♠ AJT3
♥ J6
♦ *AK93*
♣ *KQ7*

N
W   07   E
S

♠ KQ8
♥ T52
♦ 842
♣ AJ53

♠ 764
♥ A984
♦ JT5
♣ 862

Bidding:

Dealer – South	West	North	East
P	1 ♣	P	1 NT
P	3 NT	P	P
P	-	-	-

Explanation:

- West has 4 tricks and 18 HCP, so he/she opens with 1 ♣ which was aptly responded by East as 1 NT

- West has 18 HCP and knows that there is a game even if East has 9 HCP. Hence, East must bid the game at the immediate opportunity.

Bidding Example: 05

Deal No.: 01   Dealer: North   Vulnerable: None

Contract: Lead:

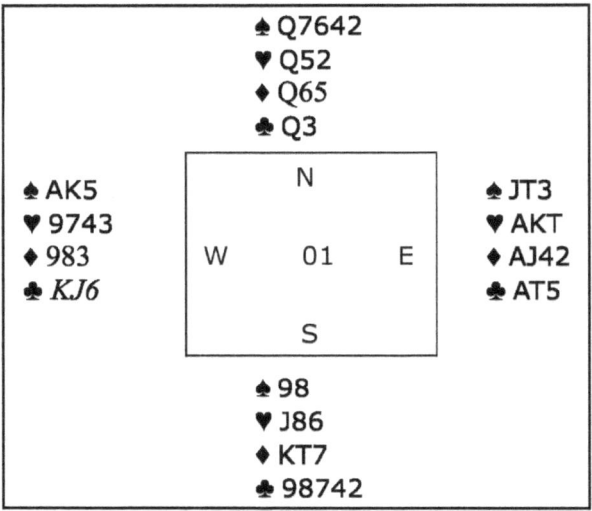

```
                  ♠ Q7642
                  ♥ Q52
                  ♦ Q65
                  ♣ Q3
    ♠ AK5            N            ♠ JT3
    ♥ 9743                        ♥ AKT
    ♦ 983     W    01    E        ♦ AJ42
    ♣ KJ6                         ♣ AT5
                    S
                  ♠ 98
                  ♥ J86
                  ♦ KT7
                  ♣ 98742
```

Bidding:

Dealer – North	East	South	West
P	1 ♣	P	I NT
P	3 NT	P	P
P	-	-	-

Explanation:

- East has 3 & ½ tricks and 17 HCP, hence opens 1 ♣.

- West has 11 HCP and responds with 1 NT.

- East knows that there is a game even if West has minimum, i.e. 9 HCP. So, he/she must jump to a game bid immediately.

Bidding Example: 06

Deal No.: 04 Dealer: West   Vulnerable: Both

Contract: Lead:

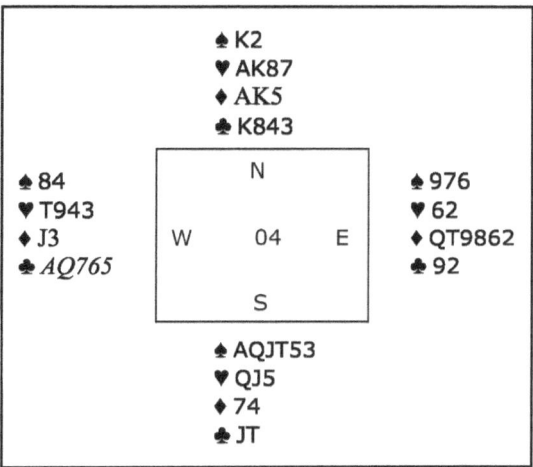

Bidding:

Dealer – West	North	East	South
P	1 ♣	P	1 ♥
P	1 NT	P	3 ♠
P	4 ♣	P	4 ♥
P	6 ♠	P	P
P	-	-	-

Explanation:

- North has 5 tricks and 20 HCP. Opens 1 ♣.
- South has 11 HCP and a six carder suit.
- North gives a waiting bid of 1 NT as the forces the partner to show his/her five carder suit.
- South has four 'honor cards' in the six carder ♠ suit. As he/she has the maximum, i.e. 11 HCP, South bids a game forcing 3 ♠.

- North only knows that the partnership has 30 - 31 HCP. North also has a double-ton King joining the partner's suit. Hence, he/she must ask Aces to explore possibility of 'Slam'. Therefore, North gives 4 ♣ as an Ace asking bid.
- South has only one Ace, hence, bids 4 ♥.
- So, the partnership has 3 Aces out of 4, but all the Kings. Hence, North bids 6 ♠, a 'Little Slam'.
- What will you do if West leads ♣ 6?

Bidding Example:07

Deal No.:03   Dealer: South   Vulnerable: E – W

Contract: Lead:

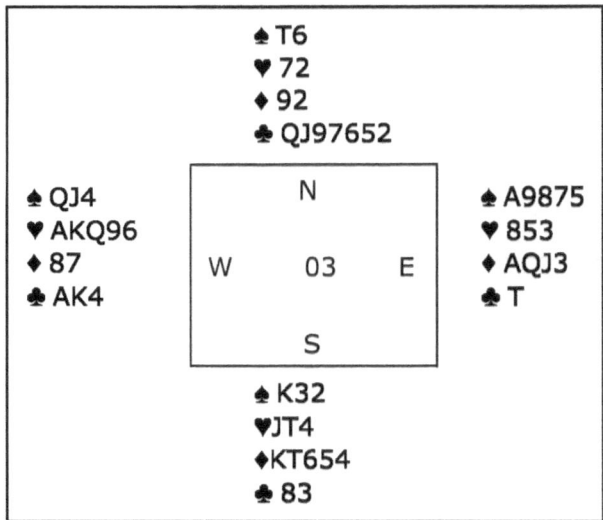

	♠ T6	
	♥ 72	
	♦ 92	
	♣ QJ97652	
♠ QJ4	N	♠ A9875
♥ AKQ96		♥ 853
♦ 87	W 03 E	♦ AQJ3
♣ AK4		♣ T
	S	
	♠ K32	
	♥ JT4	
	♦ KT654	
	♣ 83	

Bidding:

Dealer – South	West	North	East
P	1 ♣	P	1 ♥
P	3 ♥	P	3 ♠
P	4 ♣	P	4 ♠
P	5 ♣	P	5 ♦
P	6 ♠	P	P
P	-	-	-

Explanation:

- West has 4 tricks and 19 HCP. Opens with 1 ♣.
- East has 11 HCP and a five carder S. Hence, responds with 1 ♥. A part game zone.
- West gives a game force by 3 ♥.
- As East is maximum, he/she shows five carder ♠ at same level, instead of bidding 4 ♥.
- West makes an enquiry of Aces by 4 ♣ call.
- East responds 2 Aces by 4 ♠.
- West wants to know if the remaining HCP are of a King and hence makes a King asking call of 5 ♣.
- West knows that ♠ and ♦ King are missing as East responds with 5 ♦, i.e. zero Kings.
- If South doubles the 5 ♦ call by East to suggest that he/she has a ♦ suit and a King, it would become easier for West to take advantage.
- West knows that 2 or 3 discards would be available for East on his / her ♥ suit. So West can have 5 ♥ tricks, 2 ♣ tricks, 4 ♠ tricks and a ♦ trick. Hence, West bids 6 ♠, a 'Little Slam'.

Bidding Example: 08

Deal No.: 03   Dealer: South   Vulnerable: E – W

Contract: Lead:

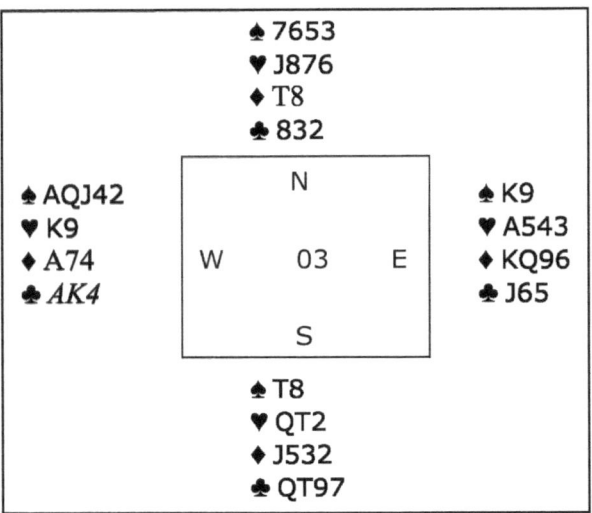

♠ 7653
♥ J876
♦ T8
♣ 832

♠ AQJ42
♥ K9
♦ A74
♣ AK4

N
W   03   E
S

♠ K9
♥ A543
♦ KQ96
♣ J65

♠ T8
♥ QT2
♦ J532
♣ QT97

Bidding:

Dealer – South	West	North	East
P	1 ♣	P	1 ♠
P	2 ♠	P	2 NT
P	4 ♣	P	4 ♥
P	5 ♣	P	5 ♠
P	6 NT	P	P
P	-	-	-

Explanation:

- West has 5 tricks and 21 HCP. Opens with 1 ♣.

- East has 13 HCP and responds with a game forcing 1 ♠.

- West shows five carder ♠ by 2 ♠.

- East denies three carder ♠ by 2 NT. Balanced hand.
- West has 21 HCP, so he/she knows that there is at least a 'Slam'.
- West makes an Ace asking bid of 4 ♣.
- East responds 1 Ace by 4 ♥.
- West makes a King asking bid by 5 ♣.
- East responds 2 Kings by 5 ♠.
- West HCP the tricks as 5 in ♠, 2 in ♥, 2 in ♦, 2 in ♣; and bids 6 NT, a 'Little Slam', hoping for either a Q in ♦ or ♣ or for trapping one of the Qs.
- Think if you can bid and make a 'Grand slam'.

Bidding Example: 09

Deal No.: 03   Dealer: South   Vulnerable: E – W

Contract: Lead:

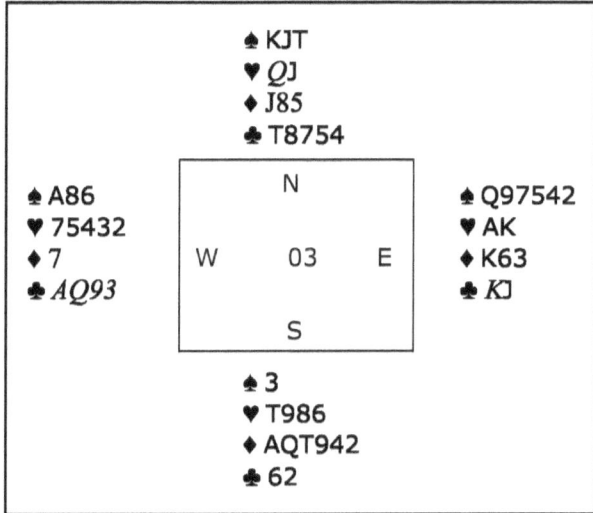

	♠ KJT	
	♥ QJ	
	♦ J85	
	♣ T8754	
♠ A86	N	♠ Q97542
♥ 75432		♥ AK
♦ 7	W 03 E	♦ K63
♣ AQ93		♣ KJ
	S	
	♠ 3	
	♥ T986	
	♦ AQT942	
	♣ 62	

Bidding:

Dealer – South	West	North	East
P	P	P	1 ♣
P	1 ♥	P	2 ♠
P	4 ♠	P	P
P	-	-	-

Explanation:

- East has 3 tricks and 16 HCP. Opens with 1 ♣.
- West has 10 HCP and a five carder ♥.
- East has to show a game force, hence, he/she bids 2 ♠.
- West is happy with three carder Ace joining East's suit. West also has 5 - 4 - 3 - 1 distribution. So he/she is happy to jump to a game.

Additional Notes:

- If East bids 1 ♠, indicating 13 - 15 HCP, then West with this hand should bid 3 ♠ instead of bidding weak five carder suit. This would be an invitation to game.
- On a 2 ♠ bid by East, if West shows any other five carder suit, then East should rebid six carder ♠. This would be invitation to a game either in 4 ♠ or in 3 NT.

Bidding Example: 10

Deal No.: 05   Dealer: North Vulnerable: N – S

Contract: Lead:

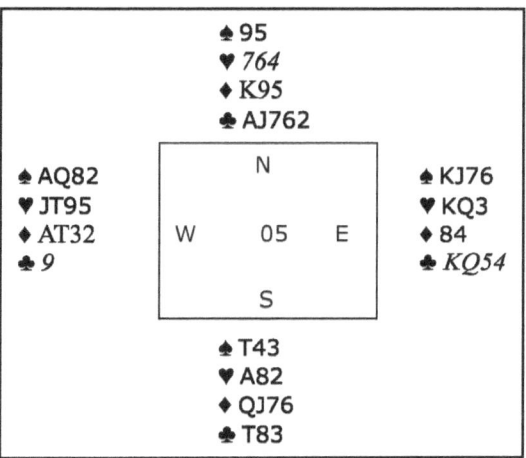

♠ 95
♥ 764
♦ K95
♣ AJ762

♠ AQ82
♥ JT95
♦ AT32
♣ 9

♠ KJ76
♥ KQ3
♦ 84
♣ KQ54

♠ T43
♥ A82
♦ QJ76
♣ T83

Bidding:

Dealer – North	East	South	West
P	1 ♣	P	2 ♣
P	3 ♠	P	4 ♠
P	P	P	-

Explanation:

- East has 2 & ½ tricks, 14 HCP and 6 pictures. Opens with 1 ♣.
- West has 11 HCP and minimum four cards in each major. Bids 2 ♣. Part game zone.
- East jumps to 3 ♠ inviting West to bid a game only if he/she has 10 - 11 HCP.

Additional Notes:

- East should bid 4 ♠ on a 2 ♣ response by West, if he/she has 15+ HCP.

- If South leads ♦ Q, West should duck it, but must cover ♦ J if played subsequently.

- Trump lead would normally help in such hands.

- Many a times, a responder has both majors but the HCP are elsewhere, and major suits are very weak. As per the convention, the hand should be responded with 2 ♣. After this response, if the opener bids a level 2 major suit, then the responder should pass. If the opener bids any other suit, in which the responder has at least doubleton, then he/she should pass.

- If on the 2 ♣ response, the opener has no major suit, and has a five carder ♣ suit with 13 - 14 HCP, he/she should pass.

Bidding Example: 11

Deal No.: 02   Dealer: East   Vulnerable: N – S

Contract: Lead:

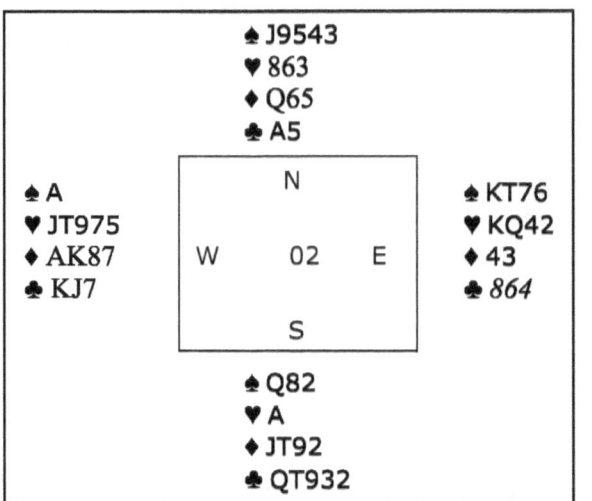

Bidding:

Dealer – East	South	West	North
P	P	1 ♣	P
2 ♣	P	4 ♥	P
P	P	-	-

Explanation:

- West has 3 & ½ tricks, 16 HCP and 6 pictures. Opens with 1 ♣.

- East has 8 HCP and both majors with four cards each. All HCP are in major suits. Hence, must bid 2 ♣, a part game zone.

- West should not want to wait. Bids a game, 4 ♥.

Additional Notes:

- Many a times, the responder has both majors but the HCP are elsewhere, and major suits are very weak. As per the convention, the hand should be responded with 2 ♣. After this response, if the opener bids level 2 major suit, then the responder should pass. If the opener bids any other suit, in which the responder has at least doubleton, then he/she should pass.

- If on the 2 ♣ response the opener has no major suit, and has a five carder ♣ suit with 13 - 14 HCP, he/she should pass.

Bidding Example: 12

Deal No.: 09 Dealer: North   Vulnerable: E – W

Contract: Lead:

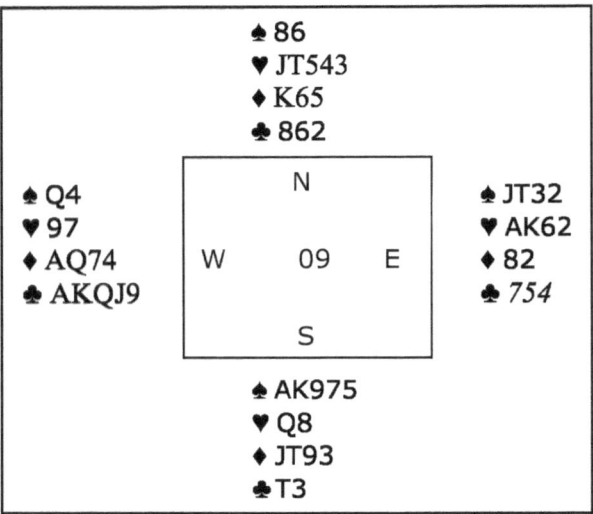

North
- ♠ 86
- ♥ JT543
- ♦ K65
- ♣ 862

West
- ♠ Q4
- ♥ 97
- ♦ AQ74
- ♣ AKQJ9

East
- ♠ JT32
- ♥ AK62
- ♦ 82
- ♣ 754

South
- ♠ AK975
- ♥ Q8
- ♦ JT93
- ♣ T3

Bidding:

Dealer – North	East	South	West
P	P	P	1 ♣
P	2 ♣	P	3 NT
P	P	P	-

Explanation:

- On a 1 ♣ opening, a response of 2 ♣ shows 8 - 11 HCP and both major suits with at least four cards in each of them.

- West has 18 HCP, a solid five card ♣ suit, positive stoppers in ♦ suit and a ♠ Q. West can also see minimum 26 HCP in both hands together. So there is a game.

- A 3 ♣ response would show five carder ♣ and would also indicate disinterest in the major suits, to be treated as a 'sign off'.

- A 2 ♦ response will indicate no major with 4 cards, minimum 3 cards in ♦ and ready to play any major, if subsequently bid by the partner. A minimum hand.

- A 3 NT bid by West assures partner that West is controlling ♣ & ♦ and has enough strength to play that contract. Therefore it is a 'sign off'.

Bidding Example: 13
Deal No.: 04   Dealer: West   Vulnerable: Both
Contract: Lead:

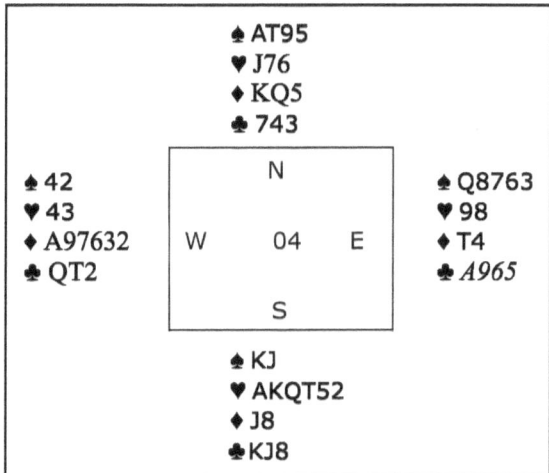

```
                    ♠ AT95
                    ♥ J76
                    ♦ KQ5
                    ♣ 743
            ┌─────────────────┐
  ♠ 42      │       N         │      ♠ Q8763
  ♥ 43      │                 │      ♥ 98
  ♦ A97632  │  W    04    E   │      ♦ T4
  ♣ QT2     │                 │      ♣ A965
            │       S         │
            └─────────────────┘
                    ♠ KJ
                    ♥ AKQT52
                    ♦ J8
                    ♣ KJ8
```

Bidding:

Dealer – West	North	East	South
P	P	P	1 ♣
P	1 NT	P	3 ♥ / 4 ♥

P	4 ♥ / P	P	P
P	-	-	-

Explanation:

- On 1 ♣ by South, North has shown 9 - 11 HCP and no five carder suit. Hence, North will generally have 3 or 2 cards in ♥. Exceptionally, North may have 4 - 4 - 4 - 1 distribution giving singleton ♥.

- On 1 NT response, a 3 ♥ bid by South would indicate 15 – 16 HCP and a conditional game force inviting North to bid a game if he/she has 10 - 11 HCP and has 3 cards of ♥ in 4 ♥ or bid 3 NT.

- In this hand South should close the bid with 4 ♥.

Bidding Example: 14

Deal No.: 08   Dealer: West   Vulnerable: None

Contract: Lead:

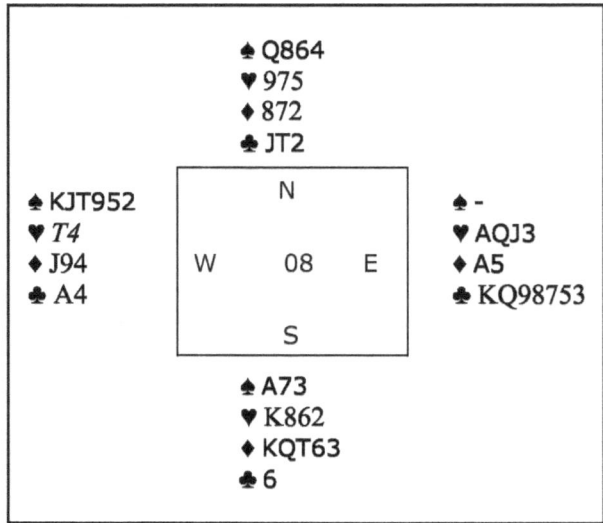

Bidding: Type 1

Dealer – West	North	East	South
P	P	1 ♣	1 ♦
1 ♠	P	3 ♣	P
3 ♠	P	3 NT	P
P	-	-	-

Bidding: Type 2 (A 'two suiter' opening)

Dealer – West	North	East	South
P	P	2 ♣	2 ♦
2 ♠	P	3 ♣	P
3 ♠	P	4 ♥	P
5 ♣	P	P	P

Explanation: In bidding type 1:

- East has 16 HCP, seven carder ♣ and four carder ♥. East would like to know the HCP strength of West as there is a solid ♣ suit.
- South has 12 HCP and gives an overcall of 1 ♦.
- West has 9 (8 - 11) HCP with minimum five cards in ♠, so must indicate the HCP strength and the suit. Since there is an intervention, West simply bids his/her suit to show 8 - 11 HCP and a five carder suit.
- East gives a game forcing suit bid by a jump in 3 ♣.
- West rebids the suit as it is a six carder.
- East gambles with 3 NT instead of showing other suit.

In bidding type 2:

- East opens 2 ♣ by showing a 'two suiter' hand with 16+ HCP, guaranteeing minimum four cards in ♣.
- South overcalls 2 ♦.

- If West passes here, it would call for the next suit by East. The 2 ♠ call indicates minimum five carder suit and 9+ HCP.
- East rebids 3 ♣ to indicate a seven carder ♣. So the other suit could be having three cards only.
- West rebids 3 ♠ to indicate a six carder suit.
- East bids 4 ♥, indicating second four carder suit and mismatch in ♠.
- West closes the contract with 5 ♣ game bid, choosing the trump suit.

Bidding Example: 15

Deal No.: 28   Dealer: West   Vulnerable: N – S

Contract: Lead:

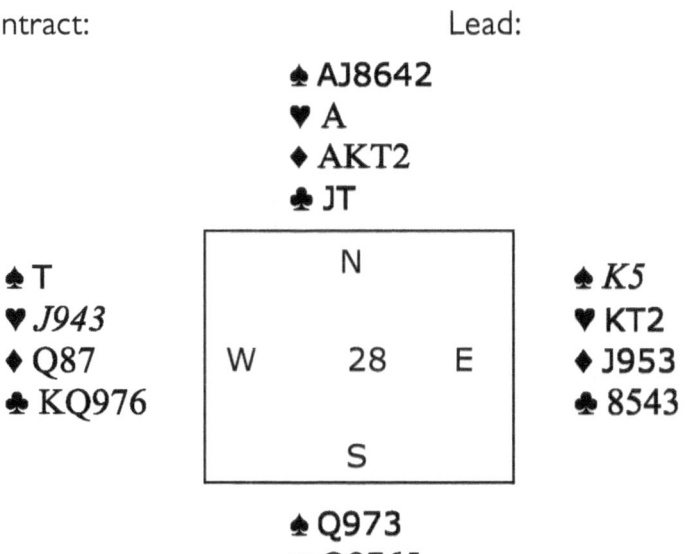

♠ AJ8642
♥ A
♦ AKT2
♣ JT

♠ T
♥ J943
♦ Q87
♣ KQ976

W   28   E

♠ K5
♥ KT2
♦ J953
♣ 8543

♠ Q973
♥ Q8765
♦ 64
♣ A2

Bidding: Type 1

Dealer – West	North	East	South
P	1 ♣	P	2 ♣
P	4 ♣	P	4 ♥
P	5 ♣	P	5 ♦
P	5 ♠	P	P
P	-	-	-

Bidding: Type 2 (A 'two suiter' opening)

Dealer – West	North	East	South
P	2 ♦	P	2 ♥
P	2 ♠	P	3 ♠
P	4 ♣	P	4 ♥
P	5 ♣	P	5 ♦
P	5 ♠	P	P

Explanation: In bidding type 1:

- North has a 'two suiter' hand with 17 HCP and would like to know the HCP strength of the partner in the first round of bidding.

- Hence North opens with 1 ♣.

- South has minimum four cards in each of the major suits with 8 (8 – 11) HCP. Hence bids 2 ♣.

- Since North has 17 HCP and a six carder join in ♠, he/she jumps to ask for Aces by 4 ♣ and Kings by 5 ♣.

- South responds 1 Ace by 4 ♥ and no Kings by 5 ♦.

- North sees minimum one loser in ♣ and may be another in ♠. Hence he/she stops the bidding with 5 ♠ call.

In bidding type 2:

- North opens a 'two suiter' hand with lower suit first as he/she is having 16+ HCP.
- South gives a relay of 2 ♥ asking the second suit.
- North shows second suit with minimum four cards as 2 ♠.
- South has a four carder ♠. Hence, he/she immediately joins with 3 ♠ bid.
- North chooses to ask Aces by 4 ♣ and Kings by 5 ♣.
- South responds 1 Ace by 4 ♥ and no Kings by 5 ♦.
- North sees minimum one loser in ♣ and may be another in ♠. Hence, he/she stops the bidding with 5 ♠ call.

Additional points:

- In North's position, one may think that he/she must know if South has three or more cards of ♠ or four or more cards of ♦ or good six or more cards in ♣, along with 8 or more HCP. In such a case, one may visualize a slam zone.
- ♠ – KQx, ♦ – QJxx, ♣ – AK, etc. with South would be the cards which can positively fetch a Grand Slam for you. When North opens 1 ♣ and if South responds 1 ♦, you must bid 2 ♠. On this opening, if South responds 1 ♥, then bid 1 ♠. On 1 ♣ opening, if South responds a game forcing 1 ♠ call, then rebid 2 ♠ and then you must take a judgment call in subsequent bidding for the correct contract.
- It would also be interesting to see how (imagine) the bidding would progress if on 1 ♣ opening by North, South responds with a 'two suiter' hand indicating 8 - 11 HCP and any two suits.

Bidding Example: 16

Deal No.: 12   Dealer: West   Vulnerable: N – S

Contract: Lead:

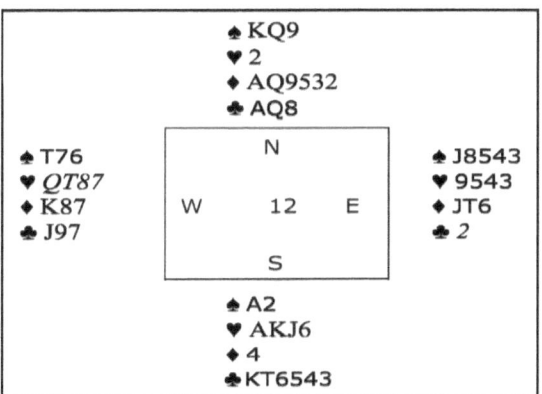

Bidding:

Dealer – West	North	East	South
P	1 ♣	P	1 ♠
P	2 ♦	P	3 ♣
P	4 ♣	P	4 ♠
P	5 ♣	P	5 ♠
P	6 ♣	P	P
P	-	-	-

Explanation:

- Opening 1 ♣ and 1 ♠ game force response are standard as per convention.

- 2 ♦ by North and 3 ♣ by South indicate minimum five carder suits.

- North has 17 HCP with 2 Aces and hence investigates Slam by 4 ♣ and 5 ♣ for Ace and King asking as he/

she joins the ♣ suit with honors such as Ace and Queen.

- A 3 ♦ response here would have indicated a six carder ♦, no three carder join in ♣ and a minimum 1 ♣ opening. Whereas, a 3 NT response would have indicated not joining in ♣ but has positive stoppers in ♥ and ♠ and a minimum opening hand. A 3 ♥/3 ♠ bid here would have indicated a five carder Diamond along with four carder bid suit.

- The opener closes at a Little Slam with 6 ♣ bid.

Bidding Example: 17

Deal No.: 10   Dealer: East   Vulnerable: Both

Contract: Lead: H King

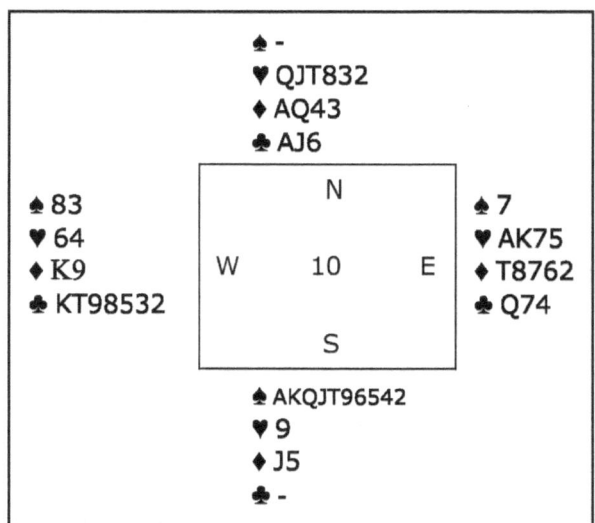

Bidding:

Dealer – East	South	West	North
P	1 ♣	P	1 ♠
P	2 ♠	P	3 ♥
Double	4 ♣	Double	4 ♦ /4 ♥
Double	6 ♠	P	P
P	-	-	-

Explanation:

- A very unusual distribution with South.

- South has 10 cards in one suit, whereas North has 10 cards in two suits.

- South sees 10 tricks single handedly with ♠ as a trump suit. So he/she decides to open with 1 ♣.

- North has 14 HCP, so responds with 1 ♠.

- South only needs to know whether North has any Aces or not and bids a 'Little Slam' in ♠. On 4 ♣ double, North should respond with 4 ♦, if he/she is playing by DOPI convention, i.e. double is zero Aces, Pass is one and 4 ♦ is two Aces.

Bidding Example: 18

Deal No.: 11   Dealer: South   Vulnerable: None

Contract: Lead:

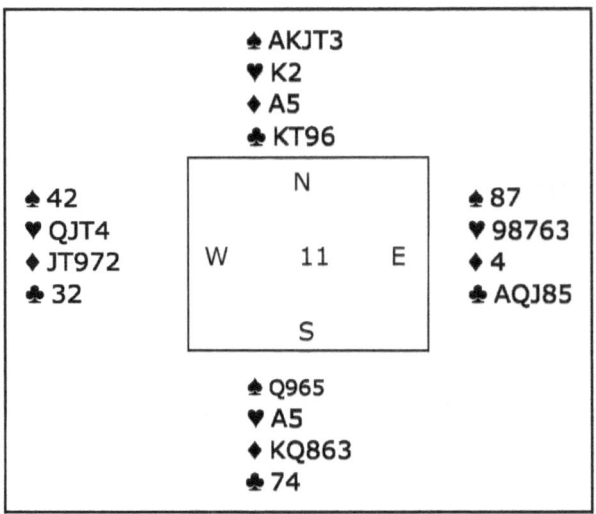

♠ AKJT3
♥ K2
♦ A5
♣ KT96

♠ 42
♥ QJT4
♦ JT972
♣ 32

W   11   E

N

S

♠ 87
♥ 98763
♦ 4
♣ AQJ85

♠ Q965
♥ A5
♦ KQ863
♣ 74

Bidding:

Dealer – South	West	North	East
P	P	1 ♣	P
1 ♥	P	2 ♠	P
4 ♣	P	4 ♠	P
5 ♣	P	5NT	P
6 ♠	P	P	P

Explanation:

- 1 ♥ response to 1 ♣ indicates 8 - 11 HCP and a five carder suit.

- 2 ♠ is a game force even if the responder has a minimum of 8 HCP and at least triple-ton ♠.

- The responder has 4 carder ♠ with a Q and 5 carder ♦ suit with KQ. Remaining suits are doubleton with an Ace of ♥.

- Hence, South makes an enquiry of Aces and Kings to find that 'Little Slam' is biddable.

- Please note that if the Aces or Kings shown are not sufficient in number, then South can stop at 4 ♠ or 5 ♠, respectively.

- If East leads ♣ Ace then, Slam is cold. If he/she leads singleton Diamond, then North should test if West discards 2 ♦ cards on 4 ♠ tricks, as South has never revealed his/her five carder suit.

Bidding Example: 19

Deal No.: 12   Dealer: West   Vulnerable: N – S

Contract: Lead:

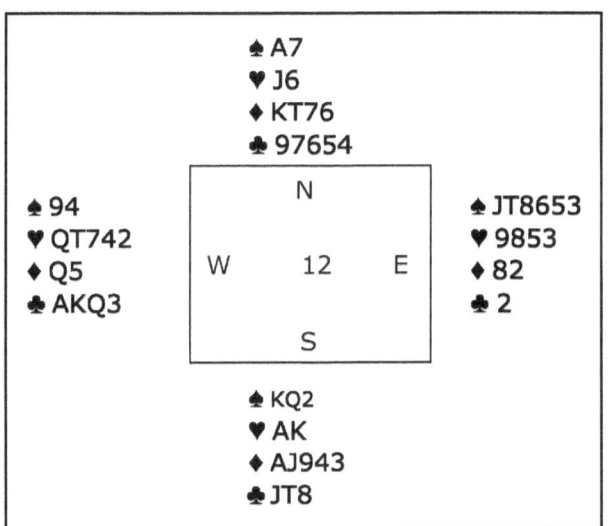

```
                  ♠ A7
                  ♥ J6
                  ♦ KT76
                  ♣ 97654
                 ┌──────────────┐
  ♠ 94          │      N       │    ♠ JT8653
  ♥ QT742       │              │    ♥ 9853
  ♦ Q5        W │     12     E │    ♦ 82
  ♣ AKQ3        │              │    ♣ 2
                 │      S       │
                 └──────────────┘
                  ♠ KQ2
                  ♥ AK
                  ♦ AJ943
                  ♣ JT8
```

Bidding: Type – 1

Dealer – West	North	East	South
P	P	P	1 ♣
P	1 ♥	P	2 ♦
P	3 ♦	P	3 NT
P	P	P	-

Bidding: Type – 2

Dealer – West	North	East	South
P	P	P	1 ♣
P	1 ♦	P	2 ♦
P	2 NT	P	3 NT
P	P	P	-

Explanation:

- North has 1 Ace and 1 King. He/she is free to bid 1 ♥ as he/she has 8 HCP, although the five carder suit is very weak minor suit and the second suit is also a minor suit.

- A 2 ♦ bid by South, on 1 ♦ response from North, if made so, indicates 16+ HCP and hence North must show 8 HCP either by bidding 2 NT or by bidding 3 NT.

Bidding Example: 20

Deal No.: 15   Dealer: South   Vulnerable: N – S

Contract: Lead:

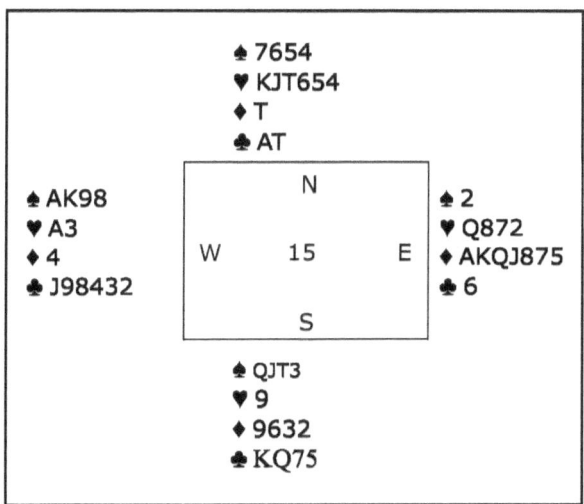

Bidding: Type – 1

Dealer – South	West	North	East
P	1 ♠	P	2 ♦
P	3 ♣	P	3 ♥
P	4 ♣	P	4 ♦
P	P	P	-

Bidding: Type – 2

Dealer – South	West	North	East
P	1 ♠	P	2 ♦
P	3 ♣	P	3 ♦
P	3 NT	P	P
P	P	P	-

Explanation:

- This is a tricky deal involving 'two suiter' hand against a 'two suiter' hand, with both the partners. Many West went by bidding sequence no. I and some of them truncated their bidding at 3 NT after East gave 3 ♥ bid. Please note that a 2 ♦ response assures 12 + HCP and a 3 ♥ bid assures four carder ♥ with a minimum 6 cards in ♦.

- In bidding sequence 2, 2 ♦ assures 12 + HCP and 3 ♦ bid assures 7 carder ♦ suit.

- 3 NT is naturally a 'gamble bid'.

- 4 ♦ is a 'par bid'.

Bidding Example: 21

Deal No.: 16   Dealer: West   Vulnerable: E – W

Contract: Lead:

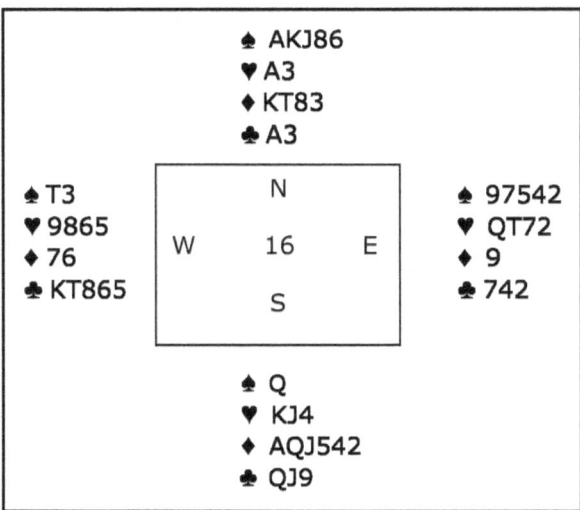

Bidding:

Dealer – West	North	East	South
P	1 ♣	P	1 ♠
P	2 ♠	P	3 ♦
P	4 ♣	P	4 ♥
P	5 ♣	P	5 ♥
P	6 ♦	P	P ?

Explanation:

- North has 4 & ½ tricks, 19 HCP and 6 pictures. Opens with 1 ♣.

- South has 16 HCP, hence responds by a game forcing 1 ♠.

- North indicates 5 carder ♠ with 2 ♠ call.

- South responds assuring five carder ♦ with 3 ♦ call.

- As North sees minimum 31 HCP in both hands together, he/she gives Ace asking bid by 4 ♣.

- South responds one Ace by 4 ♥.

- As North knows that all the Aces are with them, he/she gives a King asking bid by 5 ♣.

- South responds one King by 5 ♥.

- North shuts the bid at Little Slam, 6 ♦. He/she is worried that one King is missing. He/she can see five ♣ tricks and may be five ♠ tricks plus other two Aces.

- South passes but has a dilemma as he/she has 4 HCP more than 12, required for game forcing response and has 8 pictures, so it is more likely that both the hands together will have 14 pictures or more as Ace asking enquiry has been initiated by North promising at least 16 HCP. South could also not convey that there are 6 cards in ♦ and a singleton ♠ Q with him/her. Hence, South feels that there could be 6 ♦ tricks, 5 ♠ tricks and 2 tricks in side suits giving all 13 tricks to them, provided North has ♠ and ♣ King.

- Those Norths who analyzed as above and took a risk to bid 7 ♦, succeeded; in fact, 7 NT is a 'cold contract', which would give the highest score in a pair progressive tournament.

❑❑❑

Annexure 3

Bridge: An Intelligent Card Game for Mangers
Summary of the Engineering Bidding System

Opening Call	Meaning
1 ♣	A hand having minimum and each of : a) 2 ½ tricks b) 13 HCP, c) 5 pictures Unlimited bid
1 ♦	Hand with one of the condition a), b) & c) is not satisfied but has one suit with 5 or more cards.
1 NT	Hand with one of the condition a), b) & c) is not satisfied and has no suit with five or more cards.
NOTE: a) 1 ♣ and 1 ♦ opening calls and their first round responses are artificial. The responses are natural only when it is a two suiter response, as explained later. b) All two suiter calls are natural calls but responses to them may not be natural bids.	

I ♠, I ♥, 2 ♣, or 2 ♦	These are 'Two suiter' openings: Higher suit first, then lower - II to 15 HCP Lower suit first, then higher - 16 + HCP.
	NOTE: Prefer opening I ♣ if you have 16+ HCP and a seven carder suit.

A summary of the first responses to the above opening calls is as follows:

The first responses to the above opening calls are as given below:

Responses : To opening call of I ♣

Responses		Meaning
I ♦	0-8 HCP	Rejection.
I ♥	8-11 HCP	and having any one suit with minimum 5 cards.
I ♠	12 + HCP	Game force.
I NT	9 -11 HCP	No suit with more than 4 cards.
2 ♣	8-11 HCP	The hand guarantees both majors with at least 4 cards each.
2 ♦, 2 ♥, 2 ♠, 3 ♣	8-11 HCP	A 'two suiter' hand. The bid suit assures a minimum of 5 cards, as well as 10 Cards in two suits.

NOTE : (For the first responses)
If your Partner has opened I ♣ or I ♦ and your RHO intervenes, with a call (or Double), then Double

(Redouble) RHO's bid if you have 12+ HCP. Bid your
5 carder (or longer) suit at lowest available level if you
have 8-11 HCP (Even two suiter).

First response to the opening call of 1 ♦.

Responses		Meaning
1 ♥	0-11 HCP	Rejection.
1 ♠	12 + HCP	Game force
1 NT	9 -11 HCP	and no suit with more than 4 cards
2 ♣	8-11 HCP	Assures both majors with minimum 4 cards in each suit.
2 ♦, 2 ♥, or 2 ♠	8-11 HCP	Bid suit is the higher suit of the two suits, with minimum 5 cards in each of tham
Pass	0-7 HCP	Minimum 5 cards in the ♦ suit.

First response to the opening call of 1 NT.

Responses		Meaning
Pass	0-11 HCP	Rejection.
2 ♣	9 + HCP	Unlimited and forcing bid to ask any major suit with 4 cards.
2 ♦, 2 ♥, or 2 ♠	6-8 HCP	Five carder bid suit sign off
Pass	12-13 HCP	Normal distribution. No five card suit.
3 NT	14-15 HCP	Normal distribution
3 ♣, 3 ♦, 3 ♥ or 3 ♠	12 + HCP	Minimum 5 cards in the bid suit. Game force

First responses to two suiter opening

a) Bid next immediate suit at same level to ask opener his/her second suit.

b) Raise the level of opener's suit by one level if you have 4 cards of the suit and 6 - 8 HCP.

c) Bid NT at same level to show 9 + HCP and a balanced hand.

d) Bid a five card (or longer) suit if you have 12+ HCP.

❏❏❏

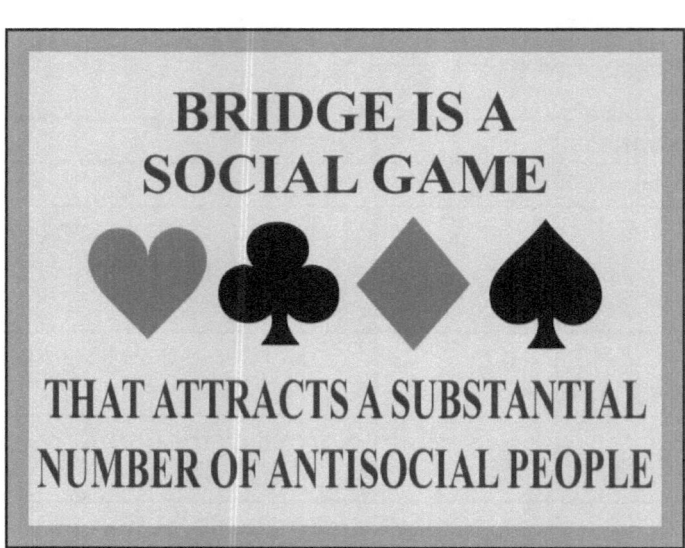

Annexure 4

Some more terms a player should know while bidding

1. **Declarer** - The bidding ends with three players bidding "Pass" (or "No-bid") after a legal call made by a player. This last call is the final contract to be played. This last bid also decides the trump. Declarer is a person who bids this trump suit first, in the auction, amongst the pair, whose last call stands as a contract.

For example – Refer bidding example 2 where West makes the last call of 4 Spade, but East becomes a declarer as he/she has bid the Spade suit first.

2. **Dummy** – When the bidding (Auction) is over, a person to the left of declarer should lead a card; face up, from his/her hand at the table and declarer's partner should put all of his/her thirteen cards, face up, on the table, arranged properly, suit wise, keeping the trump suit (if any) to his/her right side and play the cards as directed by the declarer, without making any questions or comments. So, partner of the

declarer is called as a "Dummy" and his/her cards are "Dummy – Cards".

3. **Double Dummy** – To analyze the bidding and play, you may look at all the four hands, simultaneously, by putting them, face up on the table. This is "Double Dummy" analysis or play.

4. **Jump Bid** – When it is possible for a person to bid a suit (or no-trump) at a lower level but bids at least one level above, then such a bid is called as a "Jump Bid."

For Example – RHO has bid 1 ♦ and you are free to bid Heart, Spade or NT at one level and if you still bid them at two or three level, then it is a "Jump Bid". On 1 ♦, however, you cannot bid Clubs at one level, you can bid it at two level. However, if you bid it at 'three' level, then also it becomes a 'Jump Bid'.

5. **Cue Bid** – If your RHO has bid a suit at some level and if you bid the same suit at a higher level then it is called as a "Cue Bid". Generally, it indicates that you have a first or at least second round control of the suit bid by RHO, it means you either have a singleton or void or Ace of that suit.

6. **Trumps** – The suit of the final contract is called as a "trump" suit and each card of that suit in that particular deal, is called as a "trump card". If the contract is in "No – trump" then no suit is a trump suit.

7. **Overbid** – When a call is bid which is at a higher level than the count strength (HCP) can justify or for more

tricks that one can make, even with double dummy, then the bid is said to be "overbid."

8. **Psyche or Bluff** – If a player bids a call which has a meaning (as per their convention) different than the cards held by him/her, then it is a "Bluff" or "Psyche" call. Such bids mislead opponents and at the same time the partners too. Suppose you open One Club, without having the required HCP or Tricks, then it is a "Psyche". Generally it is given with very low counts and with a favorable vulnerability.

9. **Singleton** – If you hold only one card of a particular suit, in your hand, then you are "Singleton" in that suit. Likewise, if you hold two or three cards of a particular suit, then it is a "Doubleton" or "Trippleton" suit.

10. **Void** - If you do not have any card in a particular suit then your hand is "void" in that suit.

□□□

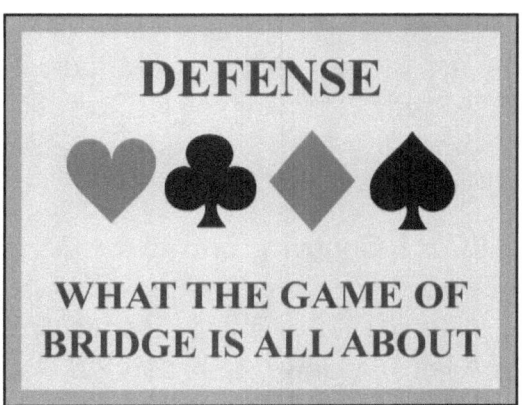

DEFENSE

WHAT THE GAME OF
BRIDGE IS ALL ABOUT

Annexure 5
Books for additional reading

Sangli District Bridge Association, Sangli, Maharashtra State (India) has maintained a library of few hundred books on the card game of "Bridge", including "Encyclopedia of Bridge".

The author has come across many books while designing this Engineering System. Some of them are,

1. **"Card Games- Properly Explained"** by Arnold Marks, Jaico Publishing House 1995

2. **"PAR – The System Without Honour, Tricks and Points"** (A study in bidding) by R. Dressler Published by the author in Nov 1950 and printed at Popular Press (Bom) Ltd.

3. **"The ABC of Contract Bridge"** by Ben Cohen & Rhoda Ledezer. Published by Vikas Publishing House Private Limited 1976, First published in 1964 by George Allen and Unwin Ltd., London

4. **"Master Bridge – by question and answers"** by Alan Truscott Vikas Publishing House Pvt. Ltd. 1979

5. **"5 Weeks To Winning Bridge"** by Alfred Sheinwold – Pocket book published by Simon & Schuster Inc. New York 10022. (1957).

❑❑❑

Special Tip 6:

Contact the author for free teaching / counselling sessions by sending an e-mail at (hkabhyankar12@rediffmail.com) with subject line Bridge & mention in body text your name and mobile number please.

About the Author

Name :   **Prof (Dr.) Hemant Keshav Abhyankar**

Education :   BE, ME (Control Systems),
                       PhD (Management)

Life member : IE(I), IETE, ISTE

Awards :   'Best Engineering College Principal' at
                       National Level, by Indian Society for
                       Technical Education, New - Delhi - 1999.

                       Praj Maha Intraprenuer Award
                       - by Praj Industries, 2009

                       Ideal Teacher Life Time Achievement
                       Award by World Peace Center (Alandi)
                       & MAEER's MIT. Best teacher awards
                       by Lions club and Rotary Club, Pune.

Ex. Principal : Sanjeevani Education Society's
                       college of engg Kopargaon.

Ex. Principal, Director
& Vice President :   Vishwakarma Institute of
                     Technology 1994 to 2015.

Exeutive Director : KJ's Educational Institute. (Eleven
                     Institutes on one campus)

Honorary Dean :   Faculty of Management, Tilak
                     Maharashtra University, Pune.

Author :   Many papers in research journals
                     A book on "Road to Engineering
                     Education ...Facts Explained."

A bridge player since 1959. Taught the game to hundreds of students, housewives and bridge lovers Participated in bridge competitions from college days in Maharashtra, Goa, Karnataka, Tamilnadu and Telangana. Offers free counselling sessions to students and Ladies.

Contact :   hkabhyankar12@rediffmail.com